Tangled Wires

LILLIAN LARK

Tangled Wires

Copyright © 2020 by Lillian Lark. All rights reserved.
No part of this book may be reproduced in any form or by any electronic or mechanical means, including information storage and retrieval systems, without written permission from the author, except for the use of brief quotations in a book review.

Editor: Kellie Montgomery
Proofreader: Rosa Sharon, My Brother's Editor

Content Warning

***

Dear Reader,
Tangled Wires has a content warning for mental illness
and suicide.
Be kind to yourselves,
L. Lark

***

To my amazing husband, the Smut Coven,
and the Relief Society.
This wouldn't have happened without you.

Prologue

Charlotte Simpson MIA for Big Company Decision
Exordium Princess, Charlotte Simpson, cancels all meetings and contact with the outside world. Sources say she hasn't been in to work and has missed the pivotal board meeting concerning the possible Vita Corp merger.

    -The Biomed Daily

Daughter of Deceased Exordium CEO/Founder on Unannounced Vacation
Exordium has released a public disclosure that Charlotte Simpson is taking a leave of absence effective immediately. A return date has not been released.

    -The Turing Herald

CEO Smith Ushering in New Merger That Keeps Exordium at the Top of Biomedical World
Matthew Smith, CEO extraordinaire, has managed the impossible and orchestrated the much-watched Vita Corp merger. The company stocks have reacted favorably to this decision and Exordium's net worth has propelled it to the most stable Biomedical company to date. Just what can't Matthew Smith accomplish?

    - The SEC Times

You'll Never Believe Where the Exordium Princess Is!

Sources say the absence of Charlotte Simpson from Exordium is expected to last exactly nine months... What exactly has this heiress been up to?

-Flash News

Clark Simpson's Daughter Returning to Exordium After Two Month Absence

Charlotte Simpson, daughter of the late renowned inventor Clark Simpson, is expected to return to Exordium and resume duties in the Research and Development branch, well-rested after taking a disconnected sabbatical.

-The Biomed Daily

Chapter 1

"*Where do you think she was?*"
"*Definitely rehab.*"

I want to roll my eyes—hard—but instead, I school my features. I pray to whichever deity will listen that this elevator ride ends soon. The blurry reflections of the women whispering behind me move, and I try not to focus on them. Their voices sound unfamiliar, but I don't want to know for sure if we're acquainted. Some might say that it's easier to navigate through life if you know friend from foe.

For me, it's both a process of elimination and a means of survival. I don't have many friends left; very few people in this company are neutral parties. They're either with me or against me. I just need to get to my office. Then I can start on my list of *I just need tos* required to get through this day.

I just need to open my email. Need to say hello to person A, respond to person B, give an analysis of how buried my desk is with various projects needing approval, and I need to avoid a certain CEO. That last one will probably be impossible. What a shame.

If the women are foes, at least they aren't smart ones. Smart foes are worse than catty women who gossip in a space the size of a closet and expect not to be overheard. I concentrate on not grinding my teeth and feel the earbuds. Oh.

That makes more sense. It's still a lot of trust to give the little devices. I had needed to blast my power song to get through all the people staring at me as I walked through the lobby. The song is over now. The silence lets the world in a little closer. Soon, the elevator will reach my floor, and then I can push the world a bit further back again.

"She doesn't look like she was pregnant."

The elevator doors reject my prayers and stay closed. I could age 100 years on this elevator ride. The doors will open, and I'll have to use a walker to leave.

"Jesus, Linda, she was only gone for two months."

"She could have gotten rid of it."

The effort it takes to pretend I don't hear them suddenly chokes me, and I remove my headphones. Thank God they instantly shut up. It isn't the first time people have spread rumors about me, and it won't be the last. My goal, entire focus today, is to get through it—rip off the Band-Aid. I don't have the energy to confront every person who regurgitates speculations about my absence.

A ping signals the end of my purgatory and the elevator doors open. Luckily, it's the right floor. Otherwise, I'd have been forced to take the stairs just to escape the incessant staring. I walk down the row of cubicles and tables scattered with different electronics and mechanical prototypes to use in bionic projects. Work ceases around me, but I ignore even more stares.

The looks on this floor burn. These are colleagues of mine. People under my management. I would have thought that they, at least, wouldn't give in to conjecture.

Some snide inner voice wonders if I should start charging for the viewing pleasure. I don't need the funds personally; Dad had left me an inheritance. But maybe I'd start a charity from it. I retract from that idea as if I've put my hand near a flame. Too soon. One thing at a time.

I finally get to my office and am accosted by *flowers?* Piles of flowers and gift baskets occupy either side of my assistant's desk.

"Ms. Simpson, it is so good to see you." Delila's cheerful Southern drawl welcomes me, and her gray bob and skirt suit almost bounce from contained happiness. The woman is the bright spot about returning to work.

"Where did all of this come from?"

Delila's smile looks a little stiff at the question.

"Your well-wishers, of course. Everyone is just so happy that you're back that they couldn't contain themselves." Her eye twitches when she says the words.

Ah, displays of fair-weather friendship. Delila's manner makes sense, for someone as genuine and loyal as she is, the machinations of the corporate atmosphere are especially bothersome. She'd worked at the company longer than I had but hadn't been exposed to the extent of fraud that is my existence here until working for me.

Delila's clear and open honesty has been more helpful than she will ever know. I thought I had been losing my mind. My past assistant had acted as if the actions of others in the company hadn't been happening. It had gone on long enough that it had been giving me a complex. *Was I misconstruing everyone else's behavior? Did that manager snub me on purpose? Were the words of that financial advisor meant to be counseling or a passive-aggressive jab?*

It was fucking exhausting, it still is. But with Delila, I know it isn't just me who interprets it this way. It had only taken one meeting to know I hadn't been making it up in my head. Delila had turned to me, fuming, before calling the manager we'd met with a *horrible man*. The kinship had been instant and invaluable.

The working situation had slowly gotten better with time. The exact time it had taken the people of the company to realize that I hadn't been given my position of managing R&D projects just because of my last name. Delila had acted as my rock in the constant storm.

"If you could arrange for these to be donated somewhere, I'd appreciate it. Maybe send one to the woman who handles our budget. She always looks like she could use a pick-me-up."

Delila raises her brows. "Ms. Sorenson? The woman who crosses herself when you walk past?"

Ouch. "Hmmm, maybe not, then." I walk toward my office door but stop with my hand on the knob. "There aren't more in my office, are there?"

A vision of being buried under gift baskets once I open the door hits me. It's ridiculous, but I'm still reassured when Delila gives a slow smile.

"Just one."

When I see the monstrosity on my desk, I want to groan. The flowers are pretty. I'll give them that. Unlike the little baskets outside, this is *an arrangement* with volume and flare. Vibrant red roses mixed with deep blue flowers I don't recognize but give a dynamic feeling to the creation. I don't have names for any of the flowers other than the roses. I'm a biomedical scientist, not a horticulturist, and the position of the arrangement across my desk is impossible to work around.

The stark white card glares at me from the front of the arrangement. The fact that this gift is in my office instead of adding to the pile outside means I don't have to check who sent it; I already know.

Still, like a masochist, I lightly pick up the expensive folded cardstock and unfold it to reveal a bold, blocky script I recognize. *He actually wrote the message himself?* Which means he must have delivered it himself. How strange, my thumb brushes over the textured paper.

Charlotte,

So good to have you back after your "sabbatical," the company just wasn't the same without you. I'm at your disposal for whatever you need. Your faithful brother.

–M

Resentment burns, topped with a healthy helping of revulsion. I crush the message into a tight ball—the edges of the card biting into my hand—but it does little to ease the sensation wrangling inside me like a small animal trying to escape. Damn. Damn. Damn. My hard-won composure begins to crack before I even sit down at my desk. I take a deep breath.

Matthew is not, nor will he ever be, my brother. It doesn't matter what story the company paints to the media to excuse the decisions in Dad's will. What does it matter to me that it's easier for the public to think that Clark Simpson hand-picked a prodigy and welcomed him into his family as a son instead of being an old eccentric who liked to play with his toys and manipulate everyone around him?

Unfortunately, it does matter. It's significant to stockholders; the stability of the company depends on the public remaining ignorant of just how off his rocker Dad was in the end. The cover story is as good as any. I'm only required to smile for the camera while next to him. It shouldn't be a hard thing to do.

That Matthew is one of the few who know where I've been the last two months disturbs me. He probably knows more about it than I do. He's the holder of all the best secrets. Sabbatical…the bastard.

Everyone knows I haven't been on a sabbatical, no matter what the press releases the company put out said. I take unholy pleasure that my return to work has ruined whichever tabloid bet on a secret baby. Most sided with the rehab story because it's the most plausible.

The wheels of industry always turn, so many professionals dabble in the endless energy source of drugs. The gossips lament and whisper that it's just so sad when they become all chewed up in the end with addiction.

Delila's voice breaks me from my thoughts. "Mr. Smith called to ask to meet with you once you were settled." She harbors a soft spot for the man, no matter that she's in her fifties; all the women who meet Matthew drool. For all of her good judgment, Delila liking Matthew rankles.

"I'll bet he did," I mutter while looking at the flowers. "Probably just wanting to welcome me back in a way that doesn't cover my desk."

Delila snickers and moves the flowers to a nearby side table, which they dwarf. I struggle to stretch my mouth into a fake smile; it's hard to keep my feelings about Matthew to myself.

Everyone adores him, and I honestly can't even blame them for falling for the lie. Matthew puts on the best show—the epitome of a young executive, smooth mannered, and quick-witted. I see him as a wolf in hiding, waiting to catch you unawares. But he's a capable wolf. Matthew has a way of negotiating through blockades that makes the shareholders look like they want to kiss him as much as Delila does.

No, I can't blame anyone because they don't know the truth.

"Well, I shouldn't keep the CEO waiting. I suppose a detour to the top floor won't put back my workload any more than it already is." I shoot a look of faux remorse at Delila. The thousands of unread emails in my inbox are only a fraction of those that passed Delila's screening measures.

My assistant grins at me. "I've already pushed your appointments for the morning, so you'll have time to review the buildup on your desk, and we can decide how to proceed once you get back."

I smile for real. Trust Delila to have all my details in order.

The floor numbers creep by while the elevator ascends. Have the elevators in this building always been so slow, or am I just that nervous? Thankfully, the elevator is empty this time. I can't remember the last time I felt like this: antsy, jumpy, sweating.

For months before the "sabbatical," I had gone to the office as a walking shell; hollow and numb. Nothing had worked for the depression that plagued me on and off again since I was a teen. I had been the inspiration for Dad's very first biomedical invention, and the company Exordium had been born from the success.

Now Exordium is an influential company, branching into all different kinds of medical devices and treatments: prosthetics, implants, surgery devices, etcetera. Clark Simpson had been the visionary who kept the company in the lead in innovation since its founding; now, they have Matthew.

I trace my index finger over the lump behind my ear almost meditative at the thought. The cranial implant that has helped millions who struggle with mental illness has never been effective for me. Now that the doctors have found the winning cocktail of medications that keep me functioning, I could get it transferred to the implant, but I won't. It feels significant every time I choose to medicate; the routine is something I do for myself, my future, to stay healthy. It is a touchstone of my recovery.

Nerves make my fidgeting worse; I really don't want to see Matthew, and the slow elevator just emphasizes that. Our past interactions haven't been great and only degraded further after Dad's death until we reached the point of not speaking; then, I rode my depression in a downward spiral until having a breakdown two months ago.

The memories of that time are a blur, but I think Matthew had visited while I was hospitalized—though, the idea that he had tortures me. It feels violating enough that he had been the one to make arrangements for my medical care.

"Why do you hate him so much?" The words had been from my main therapist Dr. Nguyen, a few weeks ago during one of our many sessions. "You've spoken of several incidents before your last downswing involving him. Yelling at him over your father's grave, arranging for his dry cleaning to be given to charity, messing with his meeting schedules. What are you trying to provoke from Mr. Smith?"

My ears had burned; summed up like that, it all seemed so petulant. It had been petulant; little ways of striking out, trying to soothe the riotous anger that seemed to pop up from nowhere and devour holes in my restraint.

I had stared at the little Zen garden in Nguyen's office instead of at the calm therapist who sat with her legs crossed as I tried to think of how to verbalize what was going on inside me. I couldn't tell her the whole truth, but I could cover the basics. Even that had felt too revealing, like a barb being yanked out of my chest.

"My father loved him more than me. Isn't that the case with most 'sibling' strife?" The words tasted bitter, but Nguyen's face showed no inflection, so I continued. "My father and I used to work on projects together after my mother died, bonding time, I guess, but then I got…sick and no longer whole. The medications to deal with my depression made my moods erratic, and my father didn't seem to want me around anymore. Hell, I didn't even know if I wanted to be around anymore."

I stopped for a breath because the memory of Dad's closed study door still ached.

"The cranial implant that he created, inspired by me, was hugely successful on the market but didn't help the situation between us." Looking back, it all seemed so simple, he had been so upset that the implant hadn't worked, hadn't fixed me. "So, he…brought in Matthew, a new protégé to lavish his attention and loving care on. One that wasn't defective, one that wouldn't yell at him for some reason or another."

Dad had gone from not wanting me around to just not wanting me anymore. I was unnecessary when he had Matthew.

"Would you define the feeling as jealousy?" Dr. Nguyen's soft words had hit like cold water.

The elevator finally dings at the top floor, making me jump. The doors open to the desk of the CEO's receptionist, which has been empty since Matthew took the CEO position. It's time to get this over with.

Matthew's office is just as stunning as the last time I'd seen it. Views of the city from the wide windows, sleek modern furniture, and masculine colors. The sharp lines fit the man. I let myself look at him lucidly for the first time in a couple of months. Matthew watches me from his spot perched on the edge of his desk, all sweeping angles and grace. Seeing him is the crescendo of returning to work. It's a bad time to notice he is more beautiful than I let myself remember. Simply put, he is perfection.

Matthew has a face reminiscent of a fallen angel, sculpted in unforgiving glory, which goes well with his steel-gray eyes and dark, fashionably cut hair. His physique is that of a swimmer with powerful shoulders and contrasting lean hips; the suit fits his long limbs perfectly, precisely. Matthew is every inch a GQ cover, but he is still a wolf, preparing to lunge for a kill. His beauty is a cruel one that scorches all that it touches, taking no prisoners, showing no mercy.

I always feel shabby next to him, a stupid feeling because I am real; a living human being, flaws included. While Matthew is an ingenious creation; designed to the very last toe hair, a contraption of moving parts, polymer-based artificial skin, 3D printed organs, and supercomputer brain. Matthew Smith is Clark Simpson's masterpiece, his pride and joy.

So, while his daughter is an unfixable type of broken, Clark had made a "son" to be gleamingly perfect, and whenever I see Matthew it's like looking into a mirror that amplifies everything about myself that Dad found less than. The lack of entrepreneurial spirit, questionable emotional stability, and every other area I had fallen short of expectation became a foundation point for Matthew's excellence.

"Lottie." Matthew's grin is sardonic and knowing; I'm staring. Embarrassment makes my face hot.

"Matty." I drop myself, unladylike, into one of the chairs in front of his desk and cross my legs. If I pop my leg, I can kick his knee at this distance. I take momentary enjoyment at the twitch of his eyebrow; he hates when I call him that as much as I dislike being called Lottie. It seems as if we are going right back to our childish ways; Nguyen would disapprove but it's almost a relief.

"Well, I just wanted to touch base. It's been a while since we've seen each other, and the last time wasn't one of your better moments."

His words are callous but the expression on his face is so stark for a moment that I'm taken aback. Why would he care?

"How are you doing, Charlotte?"

Matthew's directness makes me want to squirm. I look past him to the modern painting behind his desk before answering. The piece is the only thing in the office décor that looks organic, paints swirling with reds and blues. It resembles the flowers he left me.

"I'm good," I say.

The silence is heavy; Matthew waits, expecting. Sure, it isn't the whole truth, but it isn't his business that the stares of our coworkers are already starting to bother me even though I've been back all of five minutes. I'm not going to tell him that there had been a real temptation to call Dr. Nguyen to, once again, be reassured that I was ready to go back to work before I had even left my apartment this morning.

Most of all, I don't want to tell the beautiful usurper that I am terrified, terrified that it will all begin again, and I'll lose myself. That I'll forget to toe the line, fail to use the coping mechanisms instilled in me during recovery and be crushed underneath depression until nothing is left but the dusty numbness.

"Really Matthew, maybe you should check your programming; dial back on your motherliness. I'm not your concern." Petty, so petty, but sometimes when I open my

mouth one of the barbs that make up the tangled state of
my heart reveals itself.

At my words, Matthew's brows wing up and for some
reason, he looks pleased. "Motherliness? Is that really a trait
you think Clark gave me?"

In spite of myself, when he smiles, it takes my breath
away. That smile is lethal to me. I have a secret wrapped up
in all the complicated hang-ups of my dad's rejection.

From the time Dad started building him, Matthew
fascinated me. Clark Simpson was an undeniable genius,
leaping dozens of years ahead of current technology to build
Matthew; each attribute is impressively crafted. Each time
I came home from college I snuck into his office to see the
progress. It had been so exciting to see his creation take
shape, painful too when I realized how completely Dad had
designed him to replace me.

Professional intrigue had made me want to caress the
hardware; analyze how he was put together. That intrigue
had changed when the full program that was "Matthew"
had been uploaded. The way he had looked at me when he
was "awake" was startling. His ability to speak mockingly
one minute and have his expression soften the next, how
his program learned and adapted to improve itself. The end
product makes him seem too real.

He's not real

I have to remind myself of those simple words when just
one look from him makes my heartrate pick up. I need to
make myself believe that Matthew can't see past the veneer I
project, see that the way he speaks and moves has sensations
uncurling in my belly. Always, I have to remind myself that
he is nothing but some clever code and moving parts. Once
I remind myself of that, then I have to deal with the ugly
cognizance of wanting someone who isn't really a person.

This would usually be the point where I would lash out, maybe use ugly words, maybe pull a childish prank. Anything it took to relieve the pressure that held me in a vice, the anxiety. It isn't sane to lust after something not real and I can't do my job, won't be allowed the responsibility of designing medical devices, if I'm not sane. My job is the only thing I have left.

"I suppose that such a soft emotion wasn't high on Dad's priorities. Being able to care would make it hard to be a predator in the boardroom; ruthlessness fits much better," I muse out loud, watching as Matthew's eyes flash with an intensity that reveals his nature more so than the smile on his face.

"You're probably right in that but I'd have to first 'check my programming', as you say, to confirm it," Matthew says after staring for a pause. I realize I have been holding my breath in the face of his quiet, keeping my body still as if hoping he wouldn't see me.

Acting like prey won't achieve anything, even if the reaction felt instinctual. I force myself to project a chilly, authoritative air instead of being a deer in headlights. The man in front of me has no scruples, he wasn't designed that way.

"If we are done with this little visit, Matthew, I really need to be getting back to work, lots of catching up to be done."

Another pause, as if we are speaking in Morse code, saying more with the silence than when we break it. Matthew puts his hand over his mouth as if lost in thought, or merely trying to decide how to handle me, before throwing himself as ungracefully as I had in the armchair next to me with a sigh. I'm shocked for a moment, just like every other time he adapts his human mannerisms, except this time the gesture rings sincere.

Is the sincerity frustration? Weariness? Or is he as anxious about my coming back to work as I am?

"Charlotte," he says softly, deliberately not looking at me. "I don't want to be adversaries; I don't want it all to end up like last time. You're the only person who knows the real me and half the time you look like you want to punch me."

This is a Matthew I've never seen before. He glares toward the same modern art piece that I had when avoiding his gaze.

I take a moment to really look at him for the first time since striding into this meeting all bluster and facades. Matthew doesn't look as seamless as I remember, he looks… haggard. Can a machine look haggard or am I just projecting? Is he exposing vulnerability to crack the carefully constructed shields I've built so I can be just as easily manipulated as everyone else? It's impossible to say.

I can't let myself be fooled into the security that his openness offers. I'd be defenseless without my shields, all my wishes left naked for him to see; Matthew could destroy me if I let him in so guilelessly. I still can't help wondering… is it possible for him to be lonely?

I force my eyes back to the painting. Thinking about this makes my head and heart hurt; I won't ever get a clear answer and obsessing over something with no answer is a quick way to get a trip back to the looney bin. An insensitive and inaccurate description for a place that had provided so much help to me, but it's my own way to keep myself from sliding from my treatment plan. Dr. Nguyen would be appalled by my self-castigation, but I'm not a person who has much softness left in my spirit.

His questing fingers touch mine softly; it sears me, drawing me back to the conversation. His eyes trap me, full of as many unvoiced questions as mine are.

"So, you want what? To be friends?" My tone sounds caustic. He stiffens, pulling his fingers back under his control but his answer still lacks the usual steel of his voice.

"Friends would be nice; wouldn't you want a friend?" The yearning in his voice pulls at me, makes me want to lean closer, a human response. Until he abruptly stands and strides behind his desk, ruining the moment by continuing, "I can guarantee that you would much rather be a friend than my enemy, Charlotte."

And that's that. The return of the unflappable CEO is a relief; at least I hadn't done anything I'll regret later. Like, let myself be dragged into his web more so than I already am.

"I'll think about it." I stand with a nod, leaving the office as if I am on fire before he officially ends the meeting. Refusing to look back at the being that had always tied me up in knots. Matthew Smith is a danger to my sanity.

Chapter 2

"Oh, you're back! And so soon! It looks like you have all of your limbs still so it must not have been so bad." Delila lifts her brows cheekily. "Someone might start to think he likes you."

I'm in a daze when I return to my office but Delila's teasing shakes me from it. Her words have the barest hint of suggestion in them, softened by her drawl.

"It isn't like that." I frown. Matthew doesn't have a secret crush on me, he doesn't even like me… *does he?* I stop my thoughts before I lose any more time on this ridiculous subject. I look around the cubicles and my frown deepens. The space seems emptier; am I missing something?

"Dr. Zal is doing a demonstration in the Bio Lab. He says he's made a breakthrough on the synth skin project." Delila answers my unspoken question.

Delight sparks. "Did he really? That's fantastic news!"

Kawa had been in a stalemate on that project since before I'd taken my leave of absence. Knowing how to make the building blocks of a bio-interfacing skin but unable to solve the issue of being able to manufacture it. A frustrating cusp to ride.

Excitement buzzes under my skin but fizzles under Delila's stern look… reminding me of the pile of assignments I still need to sort through. My shoulders slouch.

Delila sighs, benevolent and haughty, "You have time to go. Dr. Zal made sure to stop by my desk and offer you the invitation."

The engineers and scientists in the Research Department step lightly around my assistant. I'd heard whispers that they consider Delila intimidating. Her job is to keep me on task. This means that she is the gatekeeper to get to me and Delila is very good at her job. She only had to exert a stern warning to a hapless engineer who barged into my office once for the rest of the department to regard her with caution.

Delila's disapproving stare packs quite a punch. Kawa must be very excited to tempt Delila's wrath.

I smile, "We'll start right when I get back."

I hurry to the Bio Lab. I use my keycard to gain access and grab a pair of safety glasses. Being back in the lab again feels like coming home. The sterile surfaces and aggressive climate control make me sigh in relief. I find the group of about ten people from my department gathered around Kawa.

Dr. Kawa Zal pulls a milky translucent product from a beaker with a ta-da gesture. It's slimy but resembles the thickness and look of skin without pigmentation. Everyone starts clapping and whooping.

Leaps in progress like this are rare and cause for celebration whether or not it is your project.

This part is why I went into engineering. The thrill of creating something completely new.

It had started the afternoon after Dad and I buried Mom. We'd come back to a quiet house, numb with grief, and Dad went straight into his workshop. It wasn't a place I'd been invited to before. Mom would say that his workshop was no place for a child, but I followed him like the lost puppy I was.

Dad jumped when he saw me, like he forgot that it was just the two of us now. We'd stared at each other for a long time. We shared the same hair color, but I took after Mom in my coloring. Dad's skin was freckled; Mom used to tease that he wasn't really blond, but a ginger in disguise. *Used to.*

It was the first time I'd seen him so tired, anguish carved in his face. It must have been startling for him to suddenly be solely responsible for a ten-year-old girl. After the staring contest, I watched Dad rub his face and sniffle.

"I guess if you're going to be in here too you should have something to do." Dad walked over to a bookshelf and picked up a thick tome before setting it down on the worktable in front of me. It read *The Electronics Handbook* and looked dusty.

He repeated the action with different items. Holding them up one at a time and naming them off until there was a pile of electronic pieces and equipment in front of me.

"You read the first two chapters of the book and I'll show you how to solder these connections," he said. All the projects after that had gone the same way. If I could get through the materials he gave me, I would get to make something. The projects increased in complexity as time went on until I started making my own projects and we'd work side by side.

Then the terrible teen years came, and I was unofficially banished from the workshop. I continued with my own projects, having been infected with the compulsion to create, and ended up studying electrical engineering at university before coming to work at Exordium.

Kawa sees me in the crowd and beams. I grin back. I don't get to create as much in my role as Chief Research Scientist now, but I still get to support some phenomenal technology.

"Ms. Simpson! I'm so glad you were able to make it!"

At his acknowledgment, the cheer of the crowds mellows but everyone is still smiling at Kawa's feat. His exuberant greeting makes me happy. We met at university and kept in touch. Kawa went on to get his PhD while I went into industry. By the time he finished with his research, I was in a position to add him to a team. We need passionate talent like his.

I'm his boss, and in front of other colleagues we act like it, but we also share something that resembles friendship. I haven't spoken to him for too long. The smile is harder to keep on my face at that thought.

"Dr. Zal, I heard you made a breakthrough and came right away. I seem to have missed the show but I'm sure I'll get a detailed report."

Kawa winks at me, "Yes, it will all be in a report. So many reports. We were able to get past the expense of having to use additive manufacturing by figuring out a molecular self-assembly method."

One of Kawa's lab partners pats him on the back, "Just think of how much more budget we'll be able to get now!"

Some of Kawa's joy dims but he nods. Kawa has been working hard to cut down on all the expenses so that the company might be able to offer the product and ensuing procedures at an affordable cost. He's the youngest in his family and all of his brothers had joined the military. One of his brothers coming home with extensive scarring had prompted the direction of Kawa's research. Exordium can serve as an avenue to provide the product to the market quicker than any other organization but there is always a price to pay.

I get closer to Kawa and bump shoulders with him. Keeping a good distance from his materials as I am sans lab coat, I lower my voice, "I'll see what I can do, okay?"

Before my breakdown, I had been in talks with several organizations that were interested in working with Exordium to get the synthetic skin released through nonprofit means. It promised to be a bloody battle with the old guard in Exordium, but it's something I wanted to work toward. Company culture be damned.

Kawa nods subdued but hopeful.

"This is fantastic progress though!" I'm not lying. Matthew's skin is synthetic, but it's a very different technology to be able to make something that can interface with existing physiology.

Kawa looks pleased, "I'm just happy to finally have progress. I know you'll try your best. Thank you, Charlotte." He raises his voice, "I'd say this is a hell of a welcome back to work!"

Chapter 3

The dark apartment cradles me in a loving embrace when I finally return to my sanctuary for the night. Keeping the lights off, I toe off my high heels and sprawl on the couch, breathing into the quiet blackness to just think. I've always enjoyed being in the dark, it's so restful compared to the light. A lit room bursts with so many things: noise, people, expectations, every reaction so loud whether physically or just my own mental musings.

Like now. If I turn on the light, there will be a to-do list of tasks, droning with monotony: take a shower, find dinner, eat dinner, etc. All things that will satisfy me physically but mentally drill away meaning through tedium. A life echoing with sameness.

I shake myself from that dismissive line of thinking. Sane thoughts, I need to think sane, stable thoughts. Not thoughts that ponder the meaning of existence because I am going to order the same food from the same restaurant yet again.

Wait, no… no food deliveries. I groan, part of my therapy specifies that food either be prepared at home or physically picked up from a restaurant, bonus points are offered if I eat at said restaurant. Ritual helps curb the worst of my hermit-like behavior but starting work has switched up my routine enough to tempt slipping back into bad habits.

Mentally I shelve thoughts of dinner, not wanting either of the allowed options. I don't need to think about that yet, I'm not hungry. Work might be a safe enough topic to allow myself to mull over.

My sigh echoes comfortably in the darkness. Today had been good, felt good. Other than the meeting with my "not-adversary" this morning, today had been about getting back in the rhythm of the projects the company had advanced in my absence. A boring but important part of my responsibilities. Soon I'd be able to indulge in what I really enjoyed, new project development.

I have goals in mind, other than going to the mats for Kawa's synthetic skin. A project in particular that I can't help being too attached to. It served as a driving factor in staying healthy. Last year was supposed to be the year. Then Dad had had his heart attack, and everything else had dulled.

Now that I have returned to work, I'll keep my plans in my back pocket, preparing for a time that I can actualize them. It would be a struggle, but I need this project. I close my eyes for a moment and try to remember his laugh, but it's been too long. *Sean.*

The trick would be how to get it done under the umbrella of Exordium.

Many of the projects the company works on involve improving failing organ systems, making the old look young, or bettering the convenience of medical methods. All those kinds of projects received unanimous shareholder approval because they pull in revenue and cater to the needs of people like them.

Anything too forward thinking faced contempt and fear. Eccentricities are better left to the work benches of mad scientists; having no place within corporations. Passion doesn't pay the bills. Innovation has the ability to become a money sink and tank a company. The board's job is to keep that from happening, hence Dad built Matthew in a basement workshop.

I roll my eyes at myself, *Matthew*. My mind reaches for him after I've restrained myself from thinking about him all day. The memory of this morning pulls me. It's gravitational, ridiculous and constant. Maybe I should take this time to unwind, process the situation. Let myself remember the expression on his face when he had spoken about wanting to be friends, the warmth of his fingers when they had softly touched mine. Or not, yeah, those thoughts aren't going anywhere healthy.

"Don't be crazy." Words spoken into the dark, annunciated with emphasis. The dark doesn't seem to have anything to say to that until a knock sounds through it, making me jump up in surprise. *Who the fuck?*

"Charlotte?"

No, Matthew cannot be outside my sanctuary. We've lived on the same floor of this building since he'd become CEO and we hadn't so much as shared an elevator ride outside of work hours. I had assumed we had been avoiding each other. Which I'd been onboard with, even if it felt ridiculous to look out the peephole before leaving my own apartment. Now, after all that effort he stands outside my door and I don't know how I want to handle this.

"Charlotte, I know you're in there… I can hear your heartbeat."

Creepy. I stumble off the couch and hit the light switch. The comfort of darkness is gone, taking my peace of mind with it. The door stands solid and I hesitate before it. I'm still in business clothes, the armor I wore today when facing him. I know how to act at work, what to expect, how to accomplish what I need. But here, in my own apartment, I feel untethered and exposed, as if Matthew snuck in through a space in the walls I'd erected.

"What are you doing here, Matthew?" My voice sounds rough to my own ears. Speaking through the door isn't good manners but… fuck it. I'm not ready to see him; opening the door would be an irrevocable action. Symbolic of starting something new. Like a coward I keep it closed.

"I bring a peace offering and some occupation for your time tonight. I got some take-out from that Indian place you're always going to," Matthew says. I perk up at the thought of curry. Getting food as a gift is a loophole to the therapy rules. Coward or not, I have to open the door; any more talking through the door would be rude… and he brought food.

"Occupation of my time?" Spoken as if I don't have plans tonight. I don't, but Matthew assuming that I have no plans hurts my ego. *Am I that predictable?*

"Well, if we're going to be friends maybe we should… hang out?"

Matthew wants to hang out; has Hell frozen over? I open the door and my brain stutters at the sight of him. He stands in the doorway mussed, suit jacket on his arm with his dress shirt sleeves rolled up. His hair looks messy, as if he's been running his fingers through it; those same fingers that had touched mine earlier.

"Are you going to let me inside?" The words purr out. I mentally curse because I'm staring, again; my face feels hot. It's clear that though I feel defenseless outside the office, Matthew does not.

"I probably won't be very good company tonight," I say. Matthew just lifts a brow, so I shrug and let Matthew the Enigma into my sanctuary; he hands over an amazing smelling bag from the curry place down the street as payment. I open the bag and the spicy steam bathes my face, the delight of it distracting me for a moment but not long. He had gotten my usual order. *How did he know?*

We don't spend time together and it wasn't like we hung out when Dad was alive. The skin on the back of my neck tickles.

"I told the owner I was picking up food for you and they packed it," Matthew says as if reading my mind or probably just deciphering the look on my face. I huff out a breath in relief and close the door of the apartment. Raj's curry is divine; I've been a regular since moving into this building and Raj always teases me good-naturedly about how I could keep him in business with just the amount of curry I order alone.

"Did you want any? Do you even like to eat food?" It's an awkward question to ask but I am, for the most part, clueless to Matthew's inner mechanics. I've seen instances where Matthew will take a bite or drink of something but it's a rare thing. I walk around Matthew, who looks around the open-plan apartment in a thoughtful way and I head for the kitchen.

"I can eat food, but I don't have to. I can also taste but it hasn't been something I've explored. Eating and drinking around people makes me seem more normal; can you imagine the reaction at work if I didn't down coffee with the rest of the masses?" Matthew muses and my abrupt laughter surprises me. It's not a sound I expected to make around him.

"With the way you work, there would definitely be a small-scale investigation of snooping coworkers trying to catch up with a, 'I'll have whatever he's having.'"

Matthew flashes me a wolfish grin. The only crack in his perfect looks is the occasional strand of dark hair falling on his cheek. That none have suspected him being more than meets the eye is miraculous.

"You should probably tone the tireless invincibility down a touch now that the worst of the company turmoil is over. People might become suspicious if you don't start to be less than perfect." I chew my lip in indecision; since when did I want to help Matthew with his deception? Probably since he looked at me in his office and asked about friendship in a way that echoed with loneliness, his edges rough and haggard.

"Actually, you have been looking less than perfect. Have you been charging your batteries? Do you need maintenance?" I slide into a comfortable clinical role to catalog his appearance.

"Trying to get a look at my hardware, Dr. Simpson?" Matthew gives an eyebrow wag and a smile of pure sin. My face burns in a blush, so effectively thrown from the clinical comfort zone, I wouldn't be surprised if I had swallowed my tongue. Jesus Christ, I'd have to go to an actual doctor soon if I keep blushing this much around him.

I admit the blushing isn't a new behavior. When Matthew and I had contact after his main program was uploaded, he always caught me blushing. It made it worse when he started trying to talk to me. He didn't say terrible things, they were nice, too nice. I started to think he must be making fun of me, so I avoided him.

But if he wanted to be friends… maybe it hadn't been a malicious sort of teasing.

"That is definitely not the way I want you handling my parts."

And now my ears burn; can ears blush? Matthew gives a wicked look and he is entirely too close; the brush of his breath catches my cheek. *When had he gotten so close?* Suddenly, overwhelmed, I rear back.

"Fuck! Anyone tell you that you're potent? I need some space. You, over there, now!" I point to the other side of the kitchen island. Matthew laughs in a way I haven't heard before, light and happy, but complies with the order. My heart beats overtime, like I'm going to implode in my own kitchen, but his laugh makes me smile even as his teasing makes my body burn.

"Maybe I need you to look closer at my linguistics?" He says the word as a sensual purr, smoothly leaning over from his banished position at the island. I snort.

"Oh my god, you need to stop." I bring my hands to my burning cheeks, but I can't stop the laughter from breaking free. When the mirth finally dissipates, my heart feels lighter than it has in a long time and my cheeks ache. Matthew smiles at me softly, as if he had accomplished what he had wanted to.

We look at each other for a moment and I have to admit that this is nice, this comradery. Maybe we really can be friends, if I can stop myself from being infatuated. Maybe Matthew will want to taste the curry; I don't think he's ever tried it before. I start to get the dishes before the food gets cold as Matthew turns to take in the apartment again.

I love my apartment; it's open and modern with high ceilings and exposed brick. The bones of the apartment are generic enough, high quality, but generic with dark wood floors and white walls I haven't bothered to add color to.

I've added colors in other ways. The fluffy multicolored throw pillows and folded blankets arranged in the space might make it look haphazard to some. There are a lot.

Every down swing, when it was the hardest for me to get out of bed, Sean and I would select another brightly colored item to add to our space. We'd spent many nights watching movie marathons in the dorms surrounded by a sea of pillows. At least the apartment gave me enough room to spread the collection out.

Photography prints are hung on all the walls. *Would he be surprised to find out they are my work?* Matthew looks at some of the small photo frames hanging up that are more sentimental than artistic.

"Is this Sean?" Matthew asks, pointing to the young man in the photo.

I flinch when he asks. It shouldn't be that much of a surprise that he knows about Sean. The photo was taken the day we'd moved into the dorms. We both look so happy. Finally leaving behind the awfulness that high school had been. Beginning a new adventure with my best friend.

"I'd rather not talk about Sean." The sting when I say that is like I cut myself. We'd just been laughing; a desperation in my chest makes me want to go back to that, not pick at old wounds. Matthew seems to understand, raising his hands as if forfeiting his line of questions. I breathe out when he goes back to taking in my place as if my freezing up never happened.

The way Matthew's shoulders lower and the fluidity of his motions give him a relaxed feel. I don't think I've ever seen him so at ease. *What does his place look like?* He wouldn't have dozens of colorful items added by caring hands. Plates in hand, I admire the layout of my place; from my spot in the kitchen I can see into the bedroom.

Suddenly, the kitchen vanishes. Matthew isn't with me. I lie under the heat of an insidious weight; the only thing that breaks the silence is the water drips. Water, that's what weighs me down with impossible gravity, that makes the idea of moving laughable. The steam wraps around my face, suffocating me, but I don't feel it. I need to do one more thing, but what is it? A question spreads through me like those ripples made from the water drops; would anyone care if I die here?

Hands grasp my arms, causing the vision to break; I'm not submerged in water anymore but gasping. Matthew's face fills my vision. He looks *off;* I've never seen the cautious intensity that writhes under the surface of his expression. I feel clammy, stomach turning in nausea. Pieces of the shattered plates litter the floor.

"What was that?" I don't mean to ask the question out loud, but I'm glad I did because Matthew's expression shutters.

"I don't know what you're talking about." Lies, he's lying to me. I don't know how I know but I do. It shouldn't surprise me that he'd lie, his entire creation and day to day actions are a lie. The illusion of a person so realistic that I keep forgetting; *he is not real.*

"Leave." Fury I hardly recognize rises in my throat. Matthew looks shocked; his hands had felt so comforting holding my arms, but with the deception make my skin crawl under his touch.

"What?" Matthew takes a step closer, as if warmth from him would soothe me but I'm having none of it.

"I want you to take your lies and leave." I thrash and his hands fall away. I take a step back.

"Charlotte, I won't lie to you—" spoken like a promise, a vow made to appeal to the neglected, lonely part of my heart. That's my weak spot, the part of me searching for a connection but I won't let my walls fall.

"Everything you are is a lie; you're not real. You're not a person, you're my father's perverse method of enforcing his will."

The violence rises in me, vitriol burning beneath the surface because an attack is all that will make up for my weak defenses against him.

Matthew looks flayed, stepping back as if I had truly broken something with the clumsy words. The look of hurt on his face makes my anger waver. We stand there in tense silence before the hurt falls from his face and Matthew does what he does best, adapts. If he can't negotiate a truce, apparently, he'll move to conquer the castle.

The movement is so quick that I couldn't have escaped if I had even thought to. Suddenly, I'm being held against Matthew's body with an arm rigidly around me as he holds my chin at an angle. His eyes are volatile, the pressure from his hand on my chin stopping just before the point of pain. Fear begins seeping through my fury.

Matthew must see that or something else on my face that makes him soften and brush a thumb over my bottom lip, lost in thought. He sighs as if pained and his hold loosens. I can pull away now, but I don't; his touch is equal parts bad and good, painful and pleasurable, terrifying and comforting.

"This isn't over, we will discuss this topic later. You go ahead and keep flinging those knives you call words, but each of us is the only person that the other can trust in this whole wide world."

He leaves, and my stomach lurches, insides confusingly sick from the truth resonating from that statement.

Chapter 4

At first glance, the bar seems empty. But first glances deceive. People come to this place to keep their own company, not to socialize. The establishment might have been described as a hole in the wall but lacks the dingy feeling for that. Instead, it just feels like a forgotten space, known only to those who need it. It's a local's bar, primarily for the corporate sort of professionals of varying ages who need to get away from what they are dealing with, whether it be at home or work.

The atmosphere reflects its clientele: subdued, tired, but clean. The décor and drinks echo those of more expensive establishments that you might try to impress a social circle with but to bring such a party here would be sacrilege. The only talking comes from quiet murmurs of those on the phone or the bartender. A good place to think, to breathe.

That's my reason for being here, to keep myself company, to think, to breathe, somewhere that isn't my apartment. Funny, how one place that usually acts as a sanctuary can also serve as a Russian roulette wheel and I don't want to get shot again tonight.

The live music provides a nice soundtrack for thoughts. Tonight, it's piano. The musician's hands move over the keys in a way that speaks of his talent. The sweet sounds make my fingers ache to play.

I try not to think too hard; the vision of the water clings to me like thorny vines. The images must be a memory, one of the many that blur together from the war of medication and severe depression that took place during my breakdown, a coiled viper waiting to strike. If I want any answers, I'll have to let Dr. Nguyen pick my brain about it. Just thinking of clinically dissecting the vivid memory makes my stomach churn.

Something I conclude without thinking too hard is that I need to apologize to Matthew for my emotional blowup. However strange his behavior had been, I can't expect him to know what is going on inside my head. Our hanging out had been… nice, before I had figuratively bitten his head off. The comfort he had offered had felt like a balm; it shined a light on just how lonely I am. The revelation leaves me emotionally raw.

Though his origins are synthetic, the feelings Matthew expresses seem as legitimate and volatile as my own. The look of hurt on his face when I had said he isn't a person haunts me. If he can experience pain, if I can hurt him with words, he is probably more of a person than I have allowed myself to consider. I would have thought myself the type of person to avoid causing another's pain; I always try to be considerate and empathetic. It's uncomfortable to realize that I have a deficiency in that consideration when it comes to Matthew.

I need to stop obsessing about the hurt I caused him. I bleed guilt; every time I think of his expression, it sinks the knife deeper.

"Penny for your thoughts?"

I jump; a man had joined me at the bar while my thoughts had drifted. The stranger is breaking the unspoken rules of this place. It makes me think he doesn't belong here. He smiles in the seductive way that a man smiles at a woman, with suggestion and promise. Two men flirting with me in one night; when did I get so popular?

I correct myself; Matthew doesn't really count as flirting. Flirting means more than just performing the actions, it requires something Matthew doesn't possess. Even if I am coming around to the idea of him being a person, robots can't desire. He can't want, not in the same way that I want when he is around. It's a depressing thought that chips at my hard-won sanity. *Chip... chip... chip.*

"My thoughts are worth more than a penny." I keep my tone cool, not wanting to invite more conversation with the interloper. The smile on the man's face grows and it surprises me to notice the stranger is rather attractive in the human way. Tousled blond hair over a slender face and a blinding smile, he wears the vintage styled frames that give his look a classy air.

"I suppose that's true; the *Exordium Princess* would have expensive thoughts."

Now there is a title I hate; the media had bestowed it on me shortly after the company had shot to success. The stranger correctly interprets my expression because he immediately throws his hands up.

"Sorry! A hazard of the job. I guess… I'm a reporter and Exordium is always a story that sells papers. But I realize I'm just playing into exactly what you must think of the media. I'm off the clock so let me start over, my name is Jim Wilson; can I buy you a drink?" Jim shoots another charming smile at me but it's a glancing blow.

I'm emotionally raw, not stupid.

"Why would a reporter want to buy me a drink unless it's to get news?" My eyes narrow at Jim, still noticing that his blazer cuts his lean figure nicely. Honest relief grows in me, relief that I can be attracted to a normal, human person with the way my mind clouds with thoughts of Matthew.

"What other reasons would a man have for buying a beautiful woman a drink?"

However unoriginal the compliment, it still has the power to make my face warm. My cautious nature tries to combat the glowing feeling that his noticing me sparks. Jim looks at me for permission; I shake my head.

"This is my last one, I have work in the morning." I swirl my glass of tonic without the gin; no alcohol for the woman on more medication than could be named in one sitting. Jim casts a dramatic look of disappointment toward me and my lips curl into a smile.

"Well, maybe you'll allow me to savor your company while you finish your drink," Jim's eyes behind his glasses spark with liveliness as his gaze traces my face. This is kind of fun; normal flirting with a normal man who is just attractive enough to make me want to take risks but not so much that he makes me catch fire.

"But whatever will we talk about?" I raise my brows in a tease before stating, "Definitely not work."

Jim laughs at that, a nice laugh.

"No, I guess we wouldn't talk about work. Yours is too secret and you would find mine too sordid. So, what do two workaholics talk about if not work?" Jim asks cheerfully.

I fight to hold on to my smile. My work habits are a matter of public opinion. The media gorges itself on whatever details they can get about me. But to have it stated so plainly still feels like a small part of my privacy is plucked away like a petal, discarded. I must keep my smile in place enough because Jim continues.

For all of Jim's complaints we find plenty to talk about; the subjects range from old movies to books but stays surface level for all the flirty dashes in between. It's a nice conversation but eventually my tonic runs dry and it's time for me to leave. Jim stands politely as I get up, running his hand down my arm, an echo of what Matthew had done earlier, sparking a sensation of déjà vu that gives me a shiver. Jim notices and slyly smiles wider before slipping me his business card.

"Let me take you for a drink sometime, I'd love to see you again." Jim grasps my fingers as he presses the card into my hand.

"I'll think about it," I muse, enjoying the thrill of flirting too much to give in so soon. Jim doesn't seem bothered by my response and flashes another confident smile before we say our farewells.

I walk the short block back to the apartment smiling from the simple interaction. Talking to Jim had been nice. I might give him a call about a date. The chemistry is mild, but I felt in complete control. It's such a departure from my thoughts about Matthew, a breath of fresh air from the shame. Maybe dating ordinary guys is what I need to stop my obsession with Matthew.

I'm climbing the stairs when the memory of the lonely dark apartment I'm headed to resurfaces past the cheer. The apartment that echoes with mysterious images just waiting to catch me off guard. I'm tempted to get a hotel room, but pride makes me keep climbing the stairs. I will not go running scared from my own home.

Entering the hallway to my floor I find that, for now, I am not alone. Matthew stands outside my door, waiting, dressed in a T-shirt and sweats; *think of the devil and he shall appear.* His apparel alone stops me in my tracks; I haven't seen him in anything but a suit for so long that this feels intimate. In the early days, when Dad was working on Matthew's programming, Matthew would meander around the workshop in similar apparel. I'd sneak glances when I could.

"So, you don't sleep in your suit?"

This moment of intimacy is… *inconvenient,* but I can't just run away. Whatever the reason he is waiting for me, I have to do the right thing. Matthew looks down at his bare toes, chagrined.

"It feels a little like being naked to be honest, but it would be unusual to wear a suit at home and normalcy is important."

He shrugs while he speaks. How exhausting it must be for him to always consider how his actions look to those around him. To have to worry about *passing. Does it bother him?*

Frustration hems me as I catch myself humanizing this android, yet again. Trying to decipher Matthew's feelings. *He's not real…*but maybe he is, if just a little bit.

"Matthew, I want to say I'm sorry. For earlier. I shouldn't have freaked out on you. Something happened in my brain, maybe a side effect of the medication; I reacted poorly and attacked you for it." My throat constricts as I try to speak calmly. Discomfort from the disorienting flashes commands me to do something, anything, to not think about them but I hold strong.

"I want to be there for you Charlotte, to be someone you can rely on. Earlier I… suspected what was going on, but I don't know how to help in a way that wouldn't make things worse. I don't want to mess up your recovery." Matthew's voice is grave; his reasoning buoys me, alleviating the worst of the paranoia. It justifies the odd expression on his face and his actions that had sparked the tinder of my already volatile emotions until they'd gone up in a blaze of fury and accusation.

We stand silently in the hallway for a moment, not quite looking at each other but not avoiding the other's eyes either. It's weird to enjoy this awkward moment, but it makes me feel less singular. Matthew produces a sound in the back of his throat as if he's going to say something but stops. He looks uncomfortably at the apartment door before settling whatever internal dialogue with a nod.

"Now that some memories are resurfacing there could be dreams… I was wondering if you would want someone around to wake you. I could sleep on your couch." His words are carefully spoken but earnest, as if he fears my reaction. If it had been the light of day I'd have refused, not wanting to appear weak to anyone, but it's night. The twisting emotions that had plagued me all day loosen at the idea of someone staying around.

"You sleep?" It's a nonanswer, but I need a minute. A minute to make sure any decision I make isn't fueled by the stark terror at the idea of being trapped in recurring memories while I sleep.

"Sometimes."

Matthew patiently rocks on his heels, not giving any more details. Earlier today, he reached out to me with an offer of friendship. If a friendship between us is going to work at all it will require effort on my part. True friendship isn't one-sided. For now, though, he's here, offering help.

"I'd like to have someone here."

I expected the words to burn. Asking for help always left a bad taste in my mouth, but it is almost a relief to accept the lifeline Matthew has thrown me. To let him be navigator of our shiny new friendship because I have no confidence that I won't steer us into a rock.

Matthew nods, not making a big deal out of the answer.

"Well then, I guess we should go to bed." Matthew lowers his voice in just the right way to make it seem both playful and suggestive. The tension that had stiffened my spine melts and all I can do is snort. With how today has gone and how daunting tomorrow seems, I'm grateful to have this man/machine at my side.

"I guess we should."

Chapter 5

I sit at the island counter in groggy disbelief watching the vision of Matthew in sweatpants, at my stove, cooking. I have to be dreaming. Seeing Matthew with sleep tousled hair messing with a frying pan makes a compelling argument that I'm still tucked away in my bed. The coffee mug in my hands grounds me in the reality that Matthew is really in my kitchen, cooking breakfast. *Since when does he cook?*

The clanging of pots and pans had woken me, and my fuzzy dreams slipped away like sand through fingers. At first, I had panicked at hearing someone else in the apartment, then I heard Matthew curse and remembered his offer the night before. My very own knight in shining armor to slay resurging memories and possible nightmares.

When Matthew had made the offer to stay on the couch, I had expected him to sneak out sometime in the early morning so that we could pretend the whole thing hadn't happened. I should have known better; he said that he wanted to be friends and Matthew does nothing in half measures.

Curiosity and the smell of coffee compelled me to the kitchen, where I now sit, ardently wishing I had donned my armor— business clothes. Or at least underwear, because God, seeing his T-shirt stretched over his back and the places his sweats cling to his sculpted body has me feeling things… Things I can usually avoid when he wears a suit. The man is temptation in the flesh. *Not a Man* not in *that* way anyway. I squeeze my thighs together and curse the revealing sleep set that I had stumbled out of my room in.

There is no missing my nipples through the light fabric, but it would be even more awkward to leave to change. That would feel like admitting something. Admitting to who? To Matthew? To myself? Confessing that I'm affected by just seeing him in my apartment means losing the battle I fight against myself. Attraction to a machine isn't healthy.

Matthew turns to me holding a plate of… "Eggs?" I ask slowly, having to guess. They hold some resemblance.

"Curtail your enthusiasm, this is my first time. I don't want to get your hopes up," Matthew pauses playfully, long enough for me to clear my throat at the double meaning and try not to blush. He continues doubtfully, "and it doesn't really look like the image on the website did…" He is right, the eggs are scrambled. Before this moment, I'd say it's a recipe that is near impossible to screw up, but these eggs… they looked sad, maybe a little soggy.

I lean over the plate to take a covert sniff. I commit to a decision and muster the determination required to follow through with my new commitment as the plate is put in front of me.

"Well, I haven't had food poisoning in a while," I say, keeping my tone light. The sad eggs smell edible enough, and it feels important that the shark of the conference room made me breakfast. Matthew freezes mid-action in a way that would have been comical if I weren't going to make myself eat the food on the plate.

"That's a joke, right? You don't think you'd really get food poisoning from this do you?" He moves to take the plate away, but I stop him. I can eat this as the peace offering it's intended as; show him that I'm interested in trying to work toward a friendship together.

"I'm joking! I'm sure it will be fine. Though, I don't really know how you got the eggs to look like this."

The tops of Matthew's ears start to turn red and I can't help but be charmed and intrigued at the mechanics of the action. Cooking and now blushing, I guess I really don't know anything about Matthew.

Matthew's sheepish grin fades as his eyes slide from my bare legs up to my sleep short hems and then the very thin tank top before reaching my face. His eyes have a glint of heat in them and my body tightens in awareness. Yes, underwear is a must next time. Maybe flannel too. Fuck it, a hoodie wouldn't hurt either.

It doesn't matter that every glance he sends communicates interest; it isn't really desire, just a good mimicry of the average red-blooded male. I just need to repeat that, over and over again, until my breath doesn't catch when he looks at me.

To distract myself from my very physical biological response, I take a large bite of eggs and promptly conclude I should have let him take them away. I chew slowly on the overly salted, greasy bits and try to come up with something to say that is complimentary. Fortunately, for my stomach, Matthew correctly reads through my poker face and blanches before snatching the plate back.

"That bad?"

I'm still chewing but shrug. *Can you really have a peace offering without a little sacrifice?*

Matthew shakes his head, thankfully not believing in suffering for peace, and slides a glass of water to me before scraping the rest of the eggs into the garbage. I grab the glass gratefully, choosing to swallow the bits down instead of chewing.

"There are breakfast bars in the cupboard," I say because I actually do want to eat this morning. Matthew's shoulders slump, dejected, but he retrieves a bar for me as I finish the coffee. At least he can manage to make a good cup of coffee. I might have kicked him out of my kitchen without caffeine to soften the rougher edges of my personality.

"Are the photos yours? I didn't know you liked photography."

Matthew stares at the framed prints decorating the walls. The one he has his eyes on might as well have been printed from my heart's blood with how close to my being it is, a black and white of my mother's grand piano. I nod with reluctance.

"Therapy mandated that I get a creative hobby when I was younger." I did grow to love photography, no matter how resistant I had been at first. My work is primarily abstract lines of buildings and similar objects. I don't take photos of people. The changeable organic natures don't appeal to my artistic eye.

"They're beautiful. Maybe you could decorate the walls of my apartment. I'll admit that my space is a little sparse." Matthew ducks his head shyly.

My curiosity is piqued by his statement. "Can you really recognize beauty in art?"

Matthew rolls his eyes, looking annoyed, "Maybe instead of questioning all the attributes that shock you, you could just assume that I'm capable of any actions I perform. When I'm with you, I'm not trying to pass for human. I'm not going to guzzle down coffee for you to look normal. If I say something is beautiful it's because I find it beautiful. I don't always know why I feel the things I do but, with you, I'm not tailoring my reactions."

My cheeks burn in embarrassment and I find myself catching a hold of his hand, squeezing.

"I'm sorry, it's the curious part of me. I've made a lot of assumptions when it comes to you and then am surprised to find I don't actually know much about you," I say.

Matthew blows out a breath, "I'm happy that you're curious about me. I want you to get to know me better. I'll try to be more obliging with your questions in the future if you try and voice them in a way that is more imploring and less in disbelief that this rickety contraption can look at something and find it beautiful."

Matthew moves his thumb in circles on my hand and raises his eyes to mine for a significant moment; my breath catches at the sensation, but Matthew continues.

"Back to the photography; I thought you already had a hobby. I'd listen to you play piano for hours. It was something I looked forward to."

So many emotions at that. Joy at the memory of playing, frustration at the circumstances around it, and pleasure that Matthew had enjoyed it. *He really didn't know?*

"I never played when my dad was home— it made him unhappy. You know my mother was a musician, the piano was hers. Dad locked it after she died. Those afternoons you heard would have been ones where I picked the lock."

Matthew's brows knit and he dips his chin.

"Well, your photography is beautiful. Maybe as enchanting as your music."

My throat constricts with his anger on his behalf, and his compliments. I don't share either skill with others very often.

I shake my head. "Thank you. Now, I'm going to get dressed for work and you should probably do the same."

I let my eyes glide over his tempting sweatpants one last time before retreating to my room.

***

When I sit down to work at my desk, the whirlwind taking up space in my mind since I woke up this morning to the beautiful, invited, intruder finally stills. The silence is a drastic departure from the loud revving of Matthew's car.

Usually I would have had a driver take me to work but since my new friend always drives, he insisted he chauffeur me while I did my best not to ask questions about his interest in flashy cars and the ability to drive. Matthew seems to legitimately enjoy his car and driving. I don't know the first thing about cars and Dad hadn't been interested in them either. Where had this interest come from?

A couple stacks of folders already crowd my desk. Delila has been busy with my requests from yesterday. The R&D team I head is capable of handling most things on their own, so I'd been able to get through most of my backlog yesterday. The only things that had been left on my docket were items that only I can sign off on or had to keep apprised of. There were a few memos that I hadn't been able to get to until today, detailing projects that Matthew had approved himself to keep them from being delayed on my behalf; it's surprising that his actions don't bother me.

The interference would have bothered me yesterday. I would have ridden the elevator, all prickly with anger, and given the micromanaging android a piece of my mind. Today, I just scan the projects, review them to ensure that they should have left the department, and conclude that Matthew's actions weren't inappropriate for the situation. It had only taken a day for Matthew to soften me up and I don't know what to think of that.

A small, paranoid part of me wonders if that's the big secret around Matthew's motives for being friendly. Lull me into complacency. It sounded so reasonable when I'd been in his office yesterday, but in the short time I've spent with him I'm getting a better picture of his personality.

That picture is probably what tempers my actions toward him. It's harder to be a bitch to someone you know, instead of the placeholder that you have of them in your mind. The strings of my emotions start to tangle whenever Matthew is involved. Even without factoring my lust into the equation, that man ties me in knots.

My phone buzzes and I check it to see a text message from Jim. A general, flirty text as a response to the text I'd sent him last night. The message only hooks my attention because of the way talking to him made me feel so normal. I hesitate a breath before sending a text back. It's shitty to use flirting with Jim to avoid the thoughts Matthew inspires but the most important thing for me is to stay in control. Even if Matthew is a person, I can't have feelings for him beyond friendship.

After finally clearing the buildup from my absence, I look at the team assignments with an alternative purpose. I pull my super-secret project up on my computer. The folder hasn't been opened for more than half a year. After Dad died, my emotional and mental state made even my day-to-day tasks too monumental to accomplish, never mind putting in the extra hours a passion project would require.

The energy required, paired with the way Dad had reacted to the concept when I'd first floated the idea, had kept the folder on my computer closed. His reaction had been… the memory is a sharp one that I try to dull with others. Memories that show Dad in a more positive light.

If I let myself revisit his ugly sneering over the project that had held my heart together, I could very easily cut the memory of Dad to ribbons. I loved him. But if I don't curate my memories from the pain he caused me, I could easily hate him too.

My project is fueled by the memory of the only person with whom my memories never cut. Sean Haddell had been my best friend. Fellow outcast of our peers. I was ostracized for the mental illness that I couldn't always hide, and he was for the physical illness that would never go away. He was the effusive, energetic partner to my subdued calm.

We had traveled the roller coaster of illness together. Some months riding high with symptoms subsiding, other months giving way to despair, but we had each other so there was always hope. Sean and I went to the same college and roomed together. Everyone thought we were a couple but that had never been the kind of love between us. We were a pair of fools entwining strings of hope that the future would bring something brighter.

I look at Sean in the hospital bed and try not to let myself cry in front of him. It helps that I'm wearing a surgical mask; no one is taking any chances of getting him sick before surgery. The mask let me pretend that Sean doesn't know how scared I am.

"Don't look at me like that Charlie." Sean smiled at me. "This is a good thing, it's what we've been hoping for."

We had been hoping for a call for the last two years. It's all we could do every time Sean had to miss classes or had to be hospitalized. Hope. Then, last night, we got the call. Sean will get his lung transplant.

"I know, I'm just… I'm so worried."

"It will be fine. The doctors know what they're doing. Pretty soon I'll be able to go jogging with you. We should plan to hike something big. Like the Appalachian Trail or something wild like that."

I laugh wetly; we've never hiked before. "Or you can finally get your nurse to go out on a date with you."

Sean points at me. "I like your idea better."

The lung transplant had gone well, and everything appeared as if it was going to finally work out. The memories of that time were bright and cheery.

The health relapse that followed had been quick and devastating. Sean was gone and I was left alone to hope, weak threads trying to hold up all the ideals we had held together. I knotted those threads until I could try to find a purpose for it all, some underlying reason that the best man I'd ever known would now be dead. I came up with nothing. Instead, I became determined to produce a purpose. If something good could come from this, maybe Sean wouldn't have died in vain.

I completed my program at school and started working for Exordium with a project in mind that would save others like Sean. Those betrayed by their DNA. Synthetic organ replacements for congenital disorders became my passion. When I had felt that the time was right, I proposed the concept to Dad.

It had not gone over well. An ugly moment with the person who had raised me.

The amount of profit for this kind of project is minimal when you factor in the cost and possible risk. Exordium needs to make money, lots of money, and that doesn't come from extreme pipe dream projects that only appeal to a fraction of the population.

Determination kindles in me; Dad isn't the ruling body of Exordium anymore. If Matthew approves the idea, this project could get off the ground. Better yet, my breath stills as a solution surfaces. An enormous amount of time could be saved in the design process if Matthew lets me use the schematics for his organs as a jumping off point.

There would have to be some big alterations to make such a schematic work in a biological body. Matthew's lungs don't perform the chemical process that lungs serve to oxygenate the blood. As far as I know, Matthew's breathing is for show. Dad had kept a lot of secrets when he was designing the android.

I hunker down to prepare the proposal, new energy in my keystrokes at the possibility of this project happening. *Finally.*

Chapter 6

"Why do you like cars?" I have to ask. Matthew smiles while expertly turning the wheel. The flashy object of his affection rumbles, the vibrations a bodily thing that makes my skin tingle. I have to admit, the car is beautiful. I have no idea about the make or model but even I can look at the sleek design and see it's engineered for speed.

My eyes take in Matthew's profile while he focuses on the road. The strong lines of his face are sharp, even turned away. When he doesn't look at me, I can admire his beauty without getting caught. The memory of his stormy gaze stays with me, but I can appreciate the way the skin around his eyes crinkles with joy.

Engineered, sleek, and powerful.

"What is not to like? The speed, the pull of the engine, all the parts working together for an exhilarating experience." He revs the engine then and my lips twitch at the pure joy on his face.

"I guess I'm curious how you like cars? Was it a programmed attribute?"

Matthew's smile falls a little and I want to kick myself.

"You don't think I can have interests cultivate organically?" Matthew counters. An interesting question. Matthew's greatest skill is his ability to adapt. It would make sense that interests could develop from adaptation through exposure.

"I guess you could. I don't know how exactly, but you can learn different skills. I don't really know what goes into evoking emotion from you." We're silent for a minute, but it's an uncomfortable minute. The air in the car feels stifling.

"Are you disappointed that I asked?" I blurt out.

Matthew's face is hard to read; he isn't smiling, his expression is more like a look of consternation. After thinking, he answers.

"I'm caught. I want to be in your company, in part, because you are the only one who knows what I really am. But whenever you ask questions trying to pick apart my personality, it feels… uncomfortable. I want you to keep asking about me because your curiosity means you're thinking about me and that makes me happy. It's all just kind of confusing for me, I guess."

When he puts it like that, the issue becomes obvious.

"You want me to think of you as a person, not a machine."

This makes his face clear and a throb of guilt tenses the muscles in my back. I had fully accepted the idea that he is a person. That my actions and questions make him feel like I don't consider him one chafes.

"Yes!" Matthew's eyes light up at that. His joy makes my transgression even worse. I've dehumanized him and haven't even noticed.

"How about a compromise?"

Matthew looks doubtful, but I soldier on. I have to do something.

"I'm interested in getting to know you, but I'm also interested in your mechanics. I don't think I can help myself from being interested from a professional standpoint."
It would be cruel to always be around an amazing

advancement in technology and never be able to know more than surface level details. "Would it work to just state I'm curious and you can fill me in on the details that you want to talk about?"

Will he feel more validated if given control of the stream of knowledge? I don't know. Can I stop putting my foot in my mouth long enough to get to know him better? Matthew looks even more doubtful, which doesn't bode well.

"You'd be okay with that? If you ask a question about my personality and I just say it is just the way I am, that wouldn't be frustrating for you?"

The imaginary scenario he suggests causes a very real bite of dissatisfaction. Matthew knows me well. I blow out a breath.

"I'm not going to lie. It will be frustrating… but if we're trying to be friends it's your right to be able to talk about the personal things you want to talk about in your own way. I'm not in charge of you."

Matthew looks thoughtful and a weight lifts from me. I might not ever know everything about how Matthew works but if he is able to talk to me about it without him feeling less than, it's worth it.

"Are you curious?" Matthew asks.

"Devastatingly," I answer, and he chuckles with a teasing glint in his eyes.

"Then I'm sure we can make plenty of compromises."

Something flutters in my chest at his sensual tease; it can't be my heart. Matthew mulls over what he wants to say.

"Clark didn't program every part of my personality as that would have taken forever. Instead, he smashed together multiple personalities he'd gathered from some other invention of his that built a program based on brain waves." Matthew makes a vague hand gesture. "And other things."

My mouth hangs open. That sounds like science fiction. Had Dad really come up with that on top of making Matthew?... Or had he *borrowed* it from a research lab? Dad wasn't one to stop progress, even if it violated morals.

"After that he made changes here and there. Iterations that he wanted." Matthew nodded like that is all there is to it. I have so many questions, but we have reached the place where Matthew has finished talking about it and I have to respect it. I make a sound but smile at him.

"This is going to be so hard."

The dry honesty makes him laugh. I'm consoled that I've finally done something right between us.

Chapter 7

Black lace floats around me like water plants in a pond, moving to tangle from some unseen force. There was a local swimming hole that my mother would take me when I was young, when the summer heat became unbearable. The underwater plants would wrap around your legs if you didn't pay attention and the water smelled like frogs, but it was my favorite place to go. I'd swim for hours while Mother sat regally under a shaded tree reading.

The black lace around my legs twines more dangerously than those water plants. Snaring me, pulling me under the warm water surrounding me. Keeping my head above the water is a struggle, my heartbeat sounds weak in my ears. I can't breathe.

I gasp awake, sitting straight up in bed. The room is dark, but familiar— my bedroom. I fall back, sinking into my pillows. My heart races, I work to take slow breaths. Happy to be able to breathe at all after the feeling of suffocation woke me. I throw an arm over my face. *A dream. Just a weird dream.*

It lacked the clarity that the first vision had but it had felt familiar enough that it could have been a part of my memories resurfacing.

These memories aren't good. They feel more like small hurts, building to something else, something full of pain. *Could that be the reason why my mind or medication has blocked them till now?* Goose bumps cover my skin. Cold, my blood feels cold in my body. The chill is persistent; I don't know how to dispel it. To sleep again.

The clacking of a keyboard from the living room has my ears perking up. *Matthew.* I hadn't wanted to wake him, which seems silly since he'd be fine without "sleep", but if he is already awake...

I put on a robe over my tank top and shorts. The material falls silkily around me and doesn't add warmth, but it helps me feel less exposed. It doesn't matter when it comes to Matthew. I can ignore the heated looks he sends me because he doesn't experience a biological desire. But covering up is what allows me to hide my reaction to him.

I smooth the robe and try to keep myself from thinking too hard at the impulse to seek him out. Sleeping right now is impossible. The sensation of drowning too fresh.

The light causes me to squint when I walk into the main area. Matthew leans back on the couch, bare feet propped on the coffee table, rapidly typing on his laptop. Seeing him so relaxed eases an unnoticed tightness in my chest. Matthew looks up from the laptop, worried.

"Are you okay?"

I only nod, suddenly shy. What do I say? I had a bad dream and want to spend some time with him? Maybe this hadn't been a good idea. I shift my weight from foot to foot trying to decide what to say or if I should just retreat into my room. Before I settle the debate, Matthew sets the laptop on the coffee table and gestures for me to sit next to him.

The offer of contact pulls me, I crave the warmth too much to turn him down. I curl up next to him on the couch. He puts an arm around me, and it's as if I'm finally connected to my physical body again after the dream. I sigh and rest my head on his shoulder.

"Thank you," I say quietly.

"Bad dream?"

The brush of his breath on my hair makes me shiver.

"Something like that. Maybe more, it's so messed up in my brain that I can't keep track of what is real and what is just a nightmare." Just saying that out loud makes me want to hide. Matthew hums and the rumble lulls me into a fragile comfort.

Our position is reminiscent of how we were a few hours ago when we watched a movie together. Our interactions had held a comfortable air up to that point. I didn't question the time we had spent together, that we had breakfast and dinner together.

It all felt so easy. Being a friend. Spending time with another person felt like exercising a muscle that had borderline atrophied from disuse. Familiar but slightly painful. Sean and I would spend hours together just keeping each other company.

I had been teasing Matthew for his movie choice, for all that his creation is the epitome of technology and he wanted to watch lightsabers, riding high on the fact that we were still getting along, when I noticed the issue of cuddling up on the couch together.

The beginning soundtrack of *Star Wars: Episode IV – A New Hope* started right as my heart rate began to pick up. I had chosen my seat next to Matthew without thought, as if I were sitting next to Sean when we had watched movies.

Sitting with the side of my body pressed against Sean's as we shared the bowl of popcorn is not the same thing as cuddling up to Matthew. His body had stiffened in surprise when I chose my seat, then he relaxed and wrapped an arm around me. It was a mistake to feel his warmth, to have our faces be so close. The contact and darkness kept my body at a low burn throughout the movie no matter how hard I tried to distract myself.

I had escaped as soon as the credits ran. Giving some excuse about being tired and going to bed early. It's not wise to guilelessly curl up in the same position that had sexually frustrated me mere hours ago, but it isn't in me to deny myself the comfort I need right now.

I try to ignore Matthew's body as I enjoy the warmth of his skin. Little by little the effects of the dream ease away. Small things begin to come to my attention, slowly changing my awareness. The heaviness of the air, the coiling tension of his body against mine. Matthew's breathing goes shallow. A shiver travels over my skin.

Curiosity draws my gaze to Matthews face and my own breathing becomes affected. Matthew looks down at me, enraptured. The tickle of the air from his breath on my breasts makes me realize that my robe and tank top gape. The fabric still clings against my nipples, a delicate barrier on sensitized skin, but he can see everything else from his vantage point. My body heats. A sensation like hot syrup flows over my skin, the sticky burn making it hard to think of anything else.

Mentally, I try to reel myself in. His reactions don't mean anything, they are only the result of a running program, a manufactured response… It isn't quite true but it's what I cling to, so my sense of logic stays afloat. But my logic quickly dissolves, sugar in water, against the bodily contact and expression of this man.

"Matthew?"

Guilty, he snaps his head up and looks away, adjusting his position on the couch with a wince that has me automatically look down. Surprise has my eyes widening and my mouth opens on its own.

"Jesus Christ, did you give yourself an upgrade? There is no way that is standard issue."

No. I did not just say that. Those words did not just come out of my mouth.

Matthew looks shocked speechless before he throws his head back in a laugh. My face is on fire. Embarrassment triggers my flight response; I lurch to leave because there is no coming back from saying something like that. Matthew pulls me into his arms, thwarting my escape, as he continues laughing at my expense.

Our bodies press against each other now since Matthew has pulled me onto his lap. He laughs into my hair. His erection presses against me. It had looked thick with the sweatpants stretched over it. The memory of it makes a sound build in my throat. I squeeze my legs together, feeling empty and slick. It turns out that being massively embarrassed does not stop one from being aroused, or it just doesn't stop me.

So many questions about what capabilities he has race through my mind. I had made some incorrect assumptions about Matthew's ability to feel desire. My body goes haywire, it doesn't help that Matthew crushes me to his chest, more in restraint than in a hug. Slowly his laughter starts to subside.

"Your fucking mouth is going to get you in trouble one of these days." His words come out as if relaxed but gravelly and I snort.

"You seem to like my mouth." I shift on his lap helplessly. Only partly able to suppress a humiliating sound as his cock swells against my ass.

Matthew chuckles darkly. "I can't deny that."

I try again to pull myself from him but it's useless with his strength holding me. "Matthew, we can't."

I don't say exactly what we can't do but the heaviness of suggestion in the air is all the context needed. My breath comes out in pants and his face nuzzles deeper into my hair.

"Why not? You seem to need something, Charlotte." His large hands rest on my outer thighs before pressing them together. The sweet pressure makes me want to weep. I'm not even surprised at his actions. This Matthew, this darker part, always thrums beneath the surface. I'd been feeling bits since the moment his programming had been loaded and had disregarded it, labeled it as past his capabilities.

"We shouldn't… You're not…" *Real? A man?* I can't finish saying it. It's ugly in this moment of sticky heat. I don't have to finish saying it because Matthew gets what I mean and squeezes my thighs together harder, cruelly evoking a pathetic sound from my throat.

"Poor little Charlotte, wanting something she's told herself she can't have." His cold growl against the back of my neck escalates my arousal to a painful point. "I can smell how wet you are. It drives me crazy. I bet if I slid my hands up these tiny shorts of yours, I'd find your pussy so hungry for this thick cock that it would beg me to sink my fingers in."

Matthew's voice is low and mean, as shame fills me and makes me burn at his filthy words because he's right. I have no control in this situation, my body is starving for this.

"...Please," am I asking for him to release me or to follow through with his sensual threat? The arch of my back argued for the latter. "I need..."

I am going to beg for him to fuck me. I've never wanted like this before and we hadn't even kissed. With just a few well-placed touches and growled words I've become a woman I don't recognize but identify as the part of me I had tried to hide ruthlessly under logic. Matthew tsks and runs a hand up my inner thigh, edging it under the shorts.

"You need... I shouldn't give you anything you need. I bet you wouldn't be begging a machine to fuck you if you weren't such a wet mess for me right now."

His hand is in my shorts now, running a finger over the sensitive, sweat damp crease of my thigh. I hold my breath, unable to speak.

His fingers softly touch my intimate folds, the wetness obvious. I gasp at the same time he huffs in frustration. An indecipherable sound comes from his chest as he works his fingers up and down, moving the wetness around. *Shouldn'ts* and *can'ts* cease to exist.

"Matthew—"

His groan interrupts my pleading.

"Say it again," Matthew orders. His raspy voice compels me into obeying. I'm under his control now, doing anything he asks just so he doesn't stop touching me.

"Matthew- Ah!" I end on a cry as two of his fingers slide deep inside me, forging ahead with an unforgiving thickness. The rest of his hand presses tauntingly against my sensitive clit.

"That's it… Good girl. You're fucking drenched," Matthew moans and I flex around his invading fingers, making both of us shudder.

"You hold me so nice and tight. Was this what you were begging for?" Matthew pumps his fingers once, a wet sound that goes with my helpless sob, I nod. I can't speak but I shift against his hard cock and Matthew rocks his hips against my ass. The sensation of his hand between my legs and his hardness against my back is too much; he must agree.

"You drive me insane Charlotte, but your pussy is fucking heaven."

"Can't be insane, that's bad," I don't even know what my mouth is saying. I could be speaking in tongues, but Matthew must know how to decipher my words because his dry laugh holds no humor.

"That isn't the type of insane I'm talking about Charlotte and you know it." *Do I?*

The depth of his fingers and his hand moving back and forth against my clit have me moaning and thrashing. His arms hold me tight against him as if to prove he can keep me here all night.

Something about the surrender of that; the inevitability of Matthew doing what he wants with me, no matter that I'd be begging him to do it, turns my thrashing to violence. His merciless fingers are so fucking deep, breathing is a luxury, I can only mewl and struggle. The feel of Matthew thrusting helplessly against my ass has me clawing at his arms. Our sex sounds fill the apartment, his grunts, my cries.

Until his teeth come down hard on my shoulder and as his cock thrusts upward, working my pussy to take his fingers even harder. The climax blinds me; I only realize I've screamed when my voice cracks. Matthew weakly moves his fingers inside me, calming me with gruff shushing sounds as we both come down.

I wince when he pulls his fingers from me but drift in the aftermath of coming hard. I don't remember the last time I'd done something as simple as orgasm. We're both breathing hard. Matthew runs his hands up and down my body, one still wet from me, his forehead resting on my shoulder where he bit down.

The wetness of Matthew's own release beneath me shocks me back to reality.

What have I done? This is the opposite of sane, opposite from everything I'm trying to do with my life now. Matthew must feel me tense and he lets his arms drop.

"You should go back to bed, Charlotte." His voice is calm but dark, a still lake of unknown depth.

Matthew isn't going to keep me here so we can talk about what we've just done. He offers space, respite, and I'm enough of a coward to take it. Self-preservation has me fleeing to my bedroom, shorts wet from his release and mine.

***

When morning breaks, I stop trying to sleep and shield myself with business clothes. I don't trust myself to walk out there in pajamas. I thought I had self-control, but it had only taken a few minutes in Matthew's presence last night to reduce me to a begging wretch. That can't happen again.

The discovery that Matthew can have a sexual desire makes this all harder. It shouldn't; all the assignation on the couch proved is that Matthew's cock worked, the ultimate replication of biology. The fact that sex is an option doesn't change anything.

The lust Matthew inspired in me isn't just a physical thing and the line between sex and emotion for me is almost nonexistent. There is no toeing this line, it's too dangerous. It isn't logical to fall in love with a machine and logic is what I use to keep from sliding into numbness.

I have to stay present, take my medication, attend my therapy, and get the synthetic lung project green lit. No matter the argument of Matthew being more than a machine, I have to focus on staying healthy. This obsession is not healthy.

I walk into the kitchen to find Matthew seated at the island, waiting for me. He wears different sweatpants than last night. Warmth tingles in my cheeks, remembering viscerally the mess he had made of that pair. His face tightens as his glance runs over the crisp slacks and blouse. Our eyes make contact and my mouth dries.

"Charlotte." Matthew nods, waiting for me to start the discussion. We need to lay this to rest. It'll be uncomfortable, but this is important. As cowardly as I was last night, I can't look Matthew in the face and say it didn't matter. That I would have done that with anyone. I can't lie, but I don't have to disclose the more harmful parts.

"Matthew."

His eyes flash at that and I need to take a breath to keep going, resisting giving ground to the memory of how he'd ordered me to say his name and how it had lit fireworks in me.

"About last night. It can't happen again." Any eloquence I wanted to summon about the situation dries in the light of day and presence of the man in front of me. Matthew gives me a hard look before tilting his head back.

"Why not?"

A simple question, asked without anger, with many faceted answers. It takes me a moment to put my answer into words that make sense without it being too convoluted with unneeded details.

"You know that my mother committed suicide?"

The look Matthew gives me confirms that of course he knows, he knows everything about me.

"People have always remarked about how alike we are. It makes sense, I guess. I look like her and she also struggled with depression throughout her life before she finally succumbed in the end."

Matthew looks like he wants to interrupt but I wave a hand and keep going.

"Since she died, I've felt the weight of everyone watching, just waiting for me to go the same way."

It hadn't been just the paparazzi, those I would have eagerly ignored. It had been people whose opinion I cared about: classmates, coworkers, the people who traveled in the same social circles. For years I've felt those eyes on me. My friendship with Sean had been the one reprieve I had from a world that kept expecting me to lose it.

"I've tried so hard to be rational, logical, to silence the whispers and gossip, but my brain chemistry always ends up sabotaging me. If I were anyone else but the daughter of the concert pianist Cordelia Simpson, the progression to my breakdown could have been different. Someone else could have received support instead of being the subject of speculation."

Even my friendship with Sean had worked against me. We had been friends for so long that my low points were thought of as normal. We'd both been young and didn't know that we should have looked out for each other in that way. We didn't know when to call for help.

"Things could have been so different if my history were different or if my dad had paid as much interest to

my mental state as the tabloids did." The pain of it all
is restricting, bound in barbed wire. "But things weren't
different, and everything became so much worse after Dad
died. Now that I do have the support I lacked, a team of
professionals that have brought me to a point of good
physical and mental health, I feel like I can breathe. I can be
sane; I can work on the things that are important to me.

"There isn't room in my life to be doing what we did last
night. You make me feel crazy, out of control, and unstable…
I just c-can't," my voice breaks on the last word. The
confession tears from me like a weed from aching earth.

Matthew's jaw is so tight when I finish that I'm surprised
by his gentleness when he takes my hand. He seems to
be battling with what to say, the draw of his eyebrows
communicating that he isn't happy about this. I bite my lips
and will myself to stay strong against his words. Finally, as if
the connection of our hands helps him, he breaks.

"You have never been insane, Charlotte."

I let out a bitter laugh before the sharp look he spears me
with silences me, he continues.

"You've had your struggles and, like you said, not nearly
enough support, but you are not your depression or your
mother. You're beautiful and talented like she was but you're
not her."

Just like that, I get choked up.

"I won't lie, I don't want to keep from touching you." His
thumb strokes over my hand in a sensual emphasis. "Making
you make those sounds… The feel of your body… Last night
was one of the best moments in my short life."

I'm shaking my head; his honesty makes this too
hard. Pulling my hand from his, I try to keep myself from
blushing or my eyes from tearing up.

Matthew sits back, the struggle showing on his face. "What do you need from me?"

The offer costs Matthew dearly from the look of intensity on his face, but it allows me to take a full breath.

"You wanted to be my friend. So, be my friend." Matthew looks away, and nods. Relief and a small part of disappointment flow through me. I suppress the disappointment; it's so much better this way. So much healthier.

Matthew sighs and the audible disappointment makes a smile kick up the corners of my mouth before he asks, "Want me to make breakfast?"

"Let's get bagels." The idea of mystery eggs is too much to handle right now. Matthew laughs.

We are so much better this way; I just need to tell myself that until I believe it.

Chapter 8

The morning light streams through the curtains, still soft at the early hour, when noises from the kitchen wake me. The sounds are a familiar part of my day now; Matthew had slept in the apartment for the past week and each morning he threw together some sort of breakfast, mostly for me, before we headed into the office. The breakfasts had marginally gotten better since that first morning. Yogurt parfait is truly impossible to mess up, but the toast was borderline inedible.

Watching Matthew struggle in the kitchen leaves me a mix of confusing emotions; the attempts cheer me up, because no matter if he burns the toast, he is doing something for me. It might be something small to other people, but I am rarely the recipient of acts with no strings attached. I'm also wary because watching him learn by trial and error is the most humanizing thing I've seen him do.

I listen to the ambient sounds of the kitchen and enjoy the warmth of the bed for a little longer. My phone vibrates on the nightstand with a text, and I smile. Jim and I have flirted back and forth since the chance meeting at the bar. It's nice to have something anchoring me in reality, something so normal. It honestly made it easier to ignore the inappropriate thoughts about Matthew. I had even agreed to go out on the date Jim had charmed me into next week. I might even go further than a date, if I can push through the betrayal that my body feels at the idea.

My body doesn't want the healthy thing. My body wants to go back to the night of the couch incident and see what else a hungry Matthew would do. The hot frustration of those thoughts drives me from my cozy place in bed. I get dressed in work clothes before going into the kitchen. Not even flannel had been enough to keep me from lusting after Matthew in the mornings, so the full armor is always in place before breakfast.

Having stalled as long as logistically feasible, I make my way into the kitchen. It isn't that I don't want to spend time with Matthew. With seeing him every morning and "hanging out" most nights, I've started to crave being around him. His wittiness, sharp commentary, and even his terrible eggs are endearing. Matthew is a good friend to have.

Unfortunately, my body still hasn't gotten the message that Matthew is a good *friend* to have. Matthew may very much be a person, but it still isn't healthy to lust after him. It can't go anywhere.

As if Matthew knows the direction of my thoughts, the smile he gives me as I walk into the kitchen is extra suggestive this morning. Luckily, Matthew wears a suit instead of the sweatpants that cling in ways that make it hard to speak in coherent sentences.

Matthew looks amazing in a suit, but a shift occurs when he wears it. This Matthew is all business. It's easier to ignore the broadness of Business Matthew's shoulders. It's what I tell myself anyway.

He puts a travel mug in my hands. "Coffee and breakfast." I breathe a sigh of relief as he hands me a breakfast bar which is generally more edible than his cooking. Matthew winks at me.

"No time for stay and chat, we have a department head meeting that got pushed to early this morning." I nod, taking a sip of the coffee. "I'll be surprised if you can get all the department heads there at the new time on a Friday morning." Generally, management did not come in during the early morning.

"Oh, they'll be there, or they'll regret it," Matthew says. His sharp smile stretches a little too wide. His blasé reaction causes me to snort; the shark is in.

* * *

I shouldn't be surprised that none of the department heads skipped out on the early meeting. They are probably terrified of pushing Matthew into making an example out of them. I'm not afraid of him, but I still wouldn't want to get on his bad side. He's vicious when he wants to be.

The Matthew of my apartment is different from the shark of the boardroom.

As the CEO, Matthew is the cold and calculating wolf who is more likely to bite your hand off than be fed from it. In my apartment he is still calculating but it's softened slightly and usually involves forcing laughter out of me. It's distracting that my body likes both. Getting hot during a meeting when Matthew sneers at the Injectables Department head for missing deadlines is not appropriate. My biology doesn't fucking care. I'll admit only to myself that I'd always been like this around Matthew.

With some determination I try to steer my thoughts to Jim when I find myself admiring Matthew for the tenth time this morning. *Think healthy thoughts, Charlotte.*

The meeting is a standard one and finishes quickly. Another attribute of working with a scarily efficient CEO is no meandering meetings. As the conference room breaks into motion, Parsons moves toward me. I mentally groan.

"Charlotte, you're looking well." Parsons had been one of my father's friends. His actions always appear above reproach, but the old guy gives me the creeps. Unfortunately, avoiding him is impossible since he heads sales.

"Yes, my sabbatical was quite refreshing." I'm surprised that I can get the words out without sounding bitter or snide but all the time I've spent with Matthew over the week has slowly drained the infection of my discontent. The discontent caused by Dad leaving Matthew the majority shares in the company, setting him up to be voted in as CEO is long gone. I didn't want the job, and Matthew is a better choice than say, Parsons.

"Yes, I'm sure it was. Such interesting timing too. So soon after your father's death. The company was in quite an upset when you went missing. The rumors were abysmal! I can't even begin to imagine what Clark would have thought of the whole affair. Not to mention the disruption it caused the synthetic skin project." Parsons's tone has quickly gone from jovial to lecturing. Did this man think that I'd, what? Be cowed by a lecture? I paste on a fake smile even if I'm concerned how much information he has about my department.

"Yes, well the synthetic skin project is actually going really well at the moment and I knew the company was in the best of hands. Matthew was the perfect person to win the position as CEO." It's a tiny jab, but effective. Parsons has been gunning for the CEO position for years and even though he'd been one of Dad's closest friends, he still doesn't know the truth about Matthew's creation. The gruff, pleasant face Parsons used to mask his true feelings sags and a bit of ugly jealousy seeps through.

"That boy—" Parsons stops, replacing his mask, and focusing on someone behind me, "Matthew! I was just speaking to Charlotte about her sabbatical. Terrible timing it was."

Now we are back on that topic. Matthew places a hand on my shoulder, a gesture that would still be in character for the "siblings" charade being played to the media, but Parsons focuses on the touch for a moment longer than necessary.

"When you need a sabbatical, you need a sabbatical. Here at Exordium it's suggested for all employees to know what they need to bring their best selves to the workplace. I hope that Charlotte's leading by example will make our employees feel capable of taking time when they need it so they can return more productive and innovative."

Parsons looks like he is about to pop a blood vessel at the pretty words Matthew spins but is trying to hide it. It's comical really, how angry he gets when the concept of work/life balance is brought up. Parsons recovers quickly.

"Well, if it's in the best interest of Exordium then it must be the right message to send." Parsons's nose flares as he doles out what he obviously thinks is bullshit. "It has been nice catching up with you Charlotte, Matthew." Nodding to us both, Parsons makes a hasty retreat. The door closes, we are alone together, and I let out a gusty sigh.

"I dislike that man," I say.

Matthew snorts and drops his hand from my shoulder, which tingles from the contact. "I couldn't tell." He moves back to where his laptop is as we both prepare to leave the conference room.

"I won't be leaving the office until later tonight, but I should be home in time for a movie, maybe *The Empire*

Strikes Back?" Matthew asks, acting like he doesn't care about my answer. I can see past this deception. Matthew has a fascination with old movies and it's been fun to experience him watching the classics for the first time.

"I'm sure I can entertain myself tonight. I did have a social life once upon a time." I promptly shut up. Maybe someday when I remember Sean, the grief won't hit me as sharply. Someday there won't be accompanying guilt from still not having the project started that I promised his memory, but today is not that day.

"I have a project that I want to talk to you about." Is now a good time? Probably not. Matthew still has the forbidding look of a predator in his natural environment. I should have brought this up at a time when Matthew is showing me his soft side, not when he's already antsy from blood in the water. His sharp eyes hold mine and I continue.

"I want to develop synthetic lungs for humans. To help people like Sean."

The look on Matthew's face is stone, immovable and solid. I force myself to go on with the pitch, trying not to let the chill of the room dissuade me.

"The market isn't just for cystic fibrosis; many other demographics need lung transplants."

Trying to lead with how many people could benefit from a product like this, could be sold a product like this.

"Charlotte—"

Matthew starts but I cut him off because I can't listen to him say no to this. Not before making a sound argument.

"We could use the plans Dad made of your lungs. I'd just need the schematics."

I'm too close to the project already, but I need this, I need for Sean's death to yield something more than my tangible grief. Matthew is the only one with access to all of Dad's research. He is already shaking his head, but I continue, desperate.

"I know a possible membrane mechanism that could oxygenate the blood to adapt it to work in a biological framework. If I could see Dad's data on how he did yours we'd be able to save years of research and development… Please, Matthew." This project is rational with sound reasoning, but Matthew's expression is pitiless. He's looking at me as if we hadn't spent the week together.

"I'm sorry, Charlotte, we can't."

Something breaks in me at his answer.

"Why not?" My cry sounds emotional, but I can't help it. *Why reject the possibility of the project if most of the R&D can be avoided?*

"Clark didn't stop and ponder whether what he was doing was right when he went about making me in his basement. He didn't stop to consider the consequences of what it would mean to have technology that would make it possible for the human race to cheat death and live forever. That was the direction of the technology that made me, Charlotte."

The idea makes my head spin. Yes, what I want, and what is possible using Dad's schematics, would extend people's lives but there is a long way between that and immortality.

"Clark didn't care that the very concept of offering immortality to the highest bidder could cause a class war. Clark just cared about doing what he wanted."

A class war. Organs for the rich. That is certainly one way to look at it.

"Dad wanted to help people," I say, but my words sound hollow. Dad wasn't a generous person. His company and innovations were centered around the profit they could bring in. Why did he create Matthew? I hadn't bothered to question before. Was it to offer immortality at a price?

"Clark was a selfish bastard who never treated you the way he should. He didn't care about saving people, he only cared about his legacy." Matthew spat the words, his face looking feral.

"My dad was a visionary!"

My mind dodges away from thinking about whatever Matthew means about how Dad treated me. What does an android know about family dynamics anyway?

"Fuck Clark, and his self-aggrandizing plans!" Matthew fumes and shock silences me. I had known, in a way, that Matthew didn't see Dad the same way that I did, but I had been ignorant to the fact that Matthew hated him. He hated his creator. That's absurd. This whole topic is wildly premature for the project on hand. I take a breath, trying to come at this from a logical perspective.

"Your position on the matter is strange as the CEO of a biomedical company."

Matthew shrugs angrily. "Exordium hasn't approached the tip of the iceberg when it comes to the kind of technology that will truly cause disruptions to the natural cycle of life."

"And you plan to what? Block any projects that would?"

His silence to the question is answer enough. Wheels spin in my mind. I don't love Exordium, it isn't my creation, nor does it feel like I own any part of it, but to purposefully hobble it goes against the grain.

"Who wouldn't do whatever it took to save a loved one from death, Charlotte? Do you think any company should be able to have that leverage?"

What would I have given for Sean not to die? Anything. I don't want to think about that, the fact that there is some truth behind Matthew's thinking.

"So, the answer to that problem is to not make technological progress? If Pandora's box stays closed there won't be any problems? How do you know that someone else won't develop this technology you fear will change the world while you're stopping Exordium from making that progress?"

"I am capable of a lot of things when it comes to technology." Matthew puts his hands in his pockets and tilts his head back; arrogant ass.

"You're going to police the whole human race? That's the grand answer for stability, stop the technology where it is?" Matthew's jaw clenches and he looks unsure for a moment before I continue. "Things aren't currently stable; they just look like it from your perspective. Technology is the great disruptor throughout history. Growth is painful, there is a cost to newness, but that newness can make things better for more people instead of just a few."

Am I the naïve one? I don't think so. I believe in responsible advancement. Would there be moments of conflict, yes. Did that mean we just stopped developing new things?

"I won't back your project, Charlotte. I won't give you my schematics either." Matthew's mouth is compressed into a thin line. He is the manifestation of stubbornness, throwing his considerable clout in the company against me. I throw my hands up. My small amount of patience is gone, replaced with helpless anger.

"Is this just another way you've decided to control me? Is that the real reason why you wanted to be friends? How far will you go to manipulate me?" My logical mind is burning. I don't even make sense to myself anymore.

"Well, someone has to stop you from making stupid decisions!"

It's like I've been smacked in the face and it must show because Matthew looks momentarily stunned by his own words.

"Charlotte, I'm so sorry, I didn't mean—"

I raise my hands as he approaches. I can't be near him right now. A hurt and cornered animal will only lash out. Who matches that description in this situation? I don't know. Disengagement is the only solution to this situation with my anger flowing over the brim.

"I'm leaving. I think we both need some space."

He doesn't try to stop me as I escape.

Chapter 9

Anger still rides me hard when I toss the project proposal for the synthetic lungs on my desk. I had typed it up but hadn't gotten around to showing it to Matthew before his obstinacy and my emotions had gotten the better of us. I never considered that Matthew would feel so strongly opposed to my passion project.

Ridiculous android!

I'm trying to remember the breathing exercises I've been taught when there is a knock at my door. John Day stands in the doorway, a little unsure in his customary bright tie and an impeccable dress shirt. The man is a proficient research engineer, even if his choice of ties makes you blink.

I had thought to add him to this project's team when it got up and running but that is going to take a lot more time than I'd planned with Matthew acting in opposition. I'll have to make sure John is placed on a challenging project in the meantime.

John is an unrepentant social climber and doesn't mind if everyone else knows that he'll leave the company if his position stalls out. Kawa has cautiously described him as someone who is hungry enough for status that he'd stand on another person's neck to get it. Not the most comfortable person to be around but he does get results.

It isn't complete nepotism that I head the Research Department. I've been at the company longer than John. But I'm aware enough that part of the reason I have stake in the company and vote on the board is that my father was Clark Simpson. Either way, I don't want to lose a promising worker like John just because a project is postponed.

"John, what can I do for you?" I stay standing. I can't bring myself to sit down yet, my adrenaline still pumps from the conflict with Matthew. John walks up to my desk, casting a look at my scattered papers as he hands me a folder.

"Delila said that you want the reports for the VEL project from January."

I flip through to check the dates and sigh in relief. "Thank you! These will help with the budgeting plan the department has to submit. Can you email a copy to both Delila and I?"

John's smile is tight, but he nods as he turns to leave.

"It's good to have you back, boss." The tone in his voice as he says goodbye makes me leery. I need to look at getting him another project soon. One more thing to handle.

I reflect on the blowup in the conference room. It's a relief to break the peace we've tiptoed around. It feels real to disagree with Matthew without him trying to cater to me, make me feel better. The whole week has felt surreal in a way. We have developed a fragile sort of relationship, getting along but avoiding all the difficult topics.

That won't cut it when cultivating a lasting relationship and I want a relationship that lasts. The night on the couch surfaces in my mind and I catch myself. A lasting *friendship*.

Matthew saying my decisions were stupid had stung... but I've probably said worse to him. I have definitely said worse to him. The personal conflict isn't the most important thing now.

Matthew doesn't want his schematics used. I mull over this new problem. Finally getting into the headspace required to think this obstacle through. If I get board approval on the project, Matthew will need to resign himself to it. Perhaps it will be easier for him to accept if I don't use his technology.

To get board approval, there needs to be at least a proof of concept that this project is possible. If I'm not going to get that from Matthew's schematic, I'll need to prototype this on my own. It would require time and equipment that couldn't be charged to the company yet. I know the perfect place to go.

***

Ivy still clings to the walls of the Tudor style mansion. For some reason that is detail I notice as the car drives down the long driveway. It takes mental focus to keep myself from flinching at the barrage of memories. All the times I had taken this same trek home to find Dad locked away in his study. I have my driver leave me at the front of the house; I don't know how long I want to be here.

Some part of me expected the old place to outwardly show the neglect, like a haunted mansion full of memories weaved together like a tangle of spider webs. A dusty dank place devoid of people but full of ghosts. It was a silly assumption. It has only been vacant for half a year; a skeleton staff would have been keeping the place maintained as any asset would have been. Things of value aren't just left to decay. In the world of the rich, neglect doesn't leave physical evidence.

No dust hangs in the air as I let myself in, no ghostly sensations trail across my nerves. It feels like any other empty, multimillion-dollar house. Devoid of personality, the expensive furniture, arranged by a decorating company, is covered with protective sheeting.

I thought I'd be sad being here, but I don't have any emotions about it other than the initial sting of Dad's rejection from his lair. I walk from room to room, looking for the one thing that I know will evoke an emotion from me, but it's the lack thereof that causes my heart to hurt. As I step into the conservatory, the empty space makes pain and disappointment radiate through me.

My mother's grand piano is gone. Maybe it was donated to a music school, or Dad had finally been able to exact in his will what he had never been able to do in his life and had the beautiful instrument destroyed. The possibility guts me, but I reel in the emotions; it was only an instrument. I dearly loved it for what it represented, not what it was. I loved to play it, maybe I should get my own.

A grand piano wouldn't fit comfortably in my modest sized apartment anyway. Disappointment needles me until I move on to a different topic. I am here for a reason. I'll get my project without Matthew's schematics and the tools in Dad's study will help my prototype development.

The door to the study is actually the door to the entire basement. As I make my way down the stairs, the dust comes off the banister to cling to my hand. Here shows the neglect I had been expecting. Even after Clark Simpson's death, the staff still abide by the rule of this place being off-limits.

Someone had packed everything up in assorted crates. It had to have been Matthew as no one else would have been allowed down here.

I had planned to take stock of what to move and hire people to help me, but the secrecy makes me rethink that. I don't want to risk Matthew's exposure. Even if we are currently fighting, we are still friends. Matthew wants to be someone I confide in, rely on.

I pull up Matthew's contact info; the call only rings once before he picks up.

"Charlotte! Are you okay?"

Confusion makes my answer slow. "Um yes, is this a bad time? Should I have texted instead?" There is a pause on the other side, and I swear I can hear Matthew breathe out slow.

"Now is good. What do you need?" he asks.

He's working late tonight. I wince and want to suddenly take back calling him.

"I'm at Dad's place to get some equipment and need some help with the heavy lifting but I just remembered that you said you were going to be at the office late today so maybe you can help me tomorrow?"

I don't want to make another trip down memory lane tomorrow but if Matthew can't make it, I'll have to wait. Another pause before Matthew answers.

"You're going to start prototyping on your own?"

"Yes, do you have a problem with that?" I ask more out of curiosity than whether he approves.

Matthew sighs, "I happen to know how stubborn you are so I don't think anything I say will make you change your mind. I'd rather go along with the ride than piss you off enough to stop talking to me. I can reschedule my meetings and be there in an hour. Does that work?"

I blink rapidly, unexplainably touched that he'd reschedule his plans for this.

We make the plans and hang up before the word to describe the fuzzy feeling in my chest comes to me; it's happiness.

Does Matthew know we just crossed a friendship bridge? The "I don't agree but I'll help you anyway" bridge.

I start to select which crates I want, their inventory recorded in Matthew's familiar blocky script. The time passes stagnantly in this place, but I hear Matthew as he comes into the basement. For a moment he just stands on the steps and takes in the dusty basement, face blank.

Is he seeing ghosts? Remembering the years that he was regulated to the basement, only ever having contact with Dad or me? With my new knowledge about Matthew that must have been terribly restricting. I hope that this place doesn't haunt him.

"Hey, thanks for coming." My words come out soft.

Seeing Matthew frozen in place, because he came when I called, softens me. We had ended on a fight last, but my anger is all but gone now. I am still frustrated with him and the views he holds about my project, but this is my closest friend and being here looks like it hurts him.

My voice breaking the silence snaps Matthew out of his remembering. He looks startled but his eyes focus on me and he takes a breath before smiling.

"Thank you for calling. After the way we left things, I didn't know if… Well, if we were going to be friends after all."

"If it was a choice between us being friends and me not getting my project, what would it be?" I want to know how he values things. His convictions about his technology or what we have together? Matthew's expression is desolate, and I think he must really value our friendship.

"Don't ask me that, Charlotte."

As if I can't already tell how much of himself he'd sacrifice at my behest just from seeing his face. I also value our friendship, but I won't stop this project just so he can be more comfortable. Since I'm not going to bother him for his schematics anymore, the point is moot.

I smile at him then with all my mushy thoughts, "Ah, I love you too, Matthew."

He looks so startled at that, I have to screw my lips to keep from laughing. Then I remember that I may be the first person to tell him something like that, even in a friendship way, and it stops my smile.

"I just want you to know you're important to me and I care about your well-being." It's uncomfortable to state it so plainly. I can feel the blush starting to tinge my cheeks.

"Enough to stop this project?"

"Don't ask that of me Matthew." I glare at him and he sighs but doesn't seem that disappointed.

"You're right, I'm sorry."

We make short work of the crates I've selected. Matthew effortlessly loads them, with his mechanical grade strength, into a SUV he had thought to bring instead of his usually flashy sports car. When he's done, he opens the passenger door for me before turning back to the house with an odd expression on his face.

"I didn't know what to do with the old place. You said you didn't want it and… I hate being here, it reminds me of being trapped in that damn basement for years but it's also where I was born."

Matthew's ill at ease expression makes me bump him with my shoulder.

"It's just a place, Matthew. We have a different place now. One we made." Consoling him is intimate, but I can't help it.

Matthew smiles at me and we leave this hollow house with mixed memories.

"Where do you want this stuff set up? This equipment won't fit in your apartment."

That is a good question. One I hadn't considered when I'd angrily come up with my plan to kick ass and take names. Matthew must see my moment of indecision.

"We can set it up at my place; it's empty enough and it's stuff that I can use when performing maintenance on myself."

His offer solves the issue he raised perfectly. Matthew not acting as an obstruction is welcome, but him actively enabling me is a gift that I didn't expect. I'm happy I called him.

"I'd really appreciate that." Something in my tone must have portrayed my thoughts because Matthew grabs my hand and squeezes it. Trying to comfort whatever emotional thing I'm dealing with.

Matthew had been right about his apartment being empty. It's bare. The walls are blindingly white, and the space looks uninhabited from the doorway except for some small plants on the kitchen island. The plants aren't even decorative, they look more like a gardening project.

I'm still pondering Matthew's apparent green thumb when I get farther into the apartment and see it. I blink at the impossibility of it. In the center of the main room is my mother's piano. I feel the tears well when I turn to look at Matthew, who just shrugs.

"It was supposed to be a surprise, I just didn't know when to surprise you with it. The walls and floor have been sound proofed, so you don't have to worry about a noise complaint. I mean, we wouldn't have to anyway since we own the building, but I figured you would have cared." Matthew

looks uncomfortable but that turns a little distressed when
the first tears begin to trail down my cheeks.

"We can move it somewhere else if you want. I just
thought you'd want to play it and it won't fit in your
apartment—"

I stop Matthew's babbling with a tight hug, tucking my
face tightly into his chest. It's the most physical contact
we've had since that night on the couch, but it's a mandatory
action for what he's given me.

"Thank you, it's wonderful."

The warmth of his body is so compelling that I need to
take a step away. The raw look in Matthew's eyes makes me
avoid his gaze.

Looking at the black, glossy instrument makes my
fingers itch. A different kind of hunger possesses me than
what usually afflicts me around Matthew.

"Do you mind?" I ask.

Matthew just grins, a quick shift of his mood, and winks
at me. "I'll finish bringing up the crates. That should give
you at least a few minutes alone to get reacquainted."

My fingers run over the key cover and I barely notice the
door clicking shut as Matthew leaves. This piano has always
bewitched me.

At first it had been because the earliest memories of my
mother had been of her fingers touching the piano keys just
so, until the sounds had magically turned into songs that
beguiled bystanders. Then she would patiently teach me to
craft the sounds into songs until I could play on my own.
We would tease each other with who would get their turn to
play and when.

After… there had been no more silly duets. I hadn't been
able to play again for years because Dad had locked the

piano. Everything had been so colorless until I had learned to pick that lock.

I arrange my hands and press the keys down. I begin to play.

The notes come to me fluidly and a song swells, sweet and potent. Before swooping down, I let myself remember all the happy memories of my mother and miss her.

Music always had a way of shining a light on my emotions, clawing the deepest ones out of the caves of my soul to be exposed to the unforgiving day. I suppose it's cathartic; even if it weren't, I don't think I would stop playing, the pain is the cost of color. It's been too long since I've let myself really feel.

Some part of me knows what resides in those caves, what I've been hiding. The people closest to me are gone: Mother, Sean, and now Dad. It's only logical that heartache would be winding me tight.

When the song ends, my face is wet, and the heaviness of grief makes me choke. Arms wrap around me in comfort. I am no longer alone in the apartment. I turn my face into the citrus scent of Matthew's dress shirt. He pulls me on his lap and cradles me as I sob.

Chapter 10

I float. I am familiar enough with this moment of disconnect to know that I'm dreaming again. The water drags at my consciousness, like the claws of a specter plucking at the strings of my existence. I remember that I've always loved Greek lore, the idea that one of the Fates is plucking at the string of my life makes my chest warm. No... not a Fate, it's the water itself that makes my chest warm.

It's both serene and terrible because there is only numbness, before and after the rain of pills… Pills? What pills? But my questions are lost to the sound of the water dripping in the tub. The drips marked the passage of time. Drip one. Drip two. Time is a fluid thing, not to be held in place by the drips of water.

I wake from the dream tense, covered in sweat and full of dread. Something about the bathtub drives me to clumsily click on the lamp on the side table, illuminating the room. Slowly, I place my wrists under the light and look closely, holding my breath. Nothing. The skin there is unblemished. My breath escapes me in a relieved gust; was it just a dream? My racing heart thinks it was real. It had felt so real.

I hadn't seen a razor in the dream, but I had heard things when I was younger, enough to know that a razor and bathtub was the way my mother committed suicide.

My hands shake as I cover my face and my eyes well. Fear, shame, and confusion beat with my erratic heart. Was it a nightmare? Some lurking mental hang-ups about my mother? I breathe, searching for calm.

I'll bring it up with Nguyen later. I frown; I haven't checked in with her in a while. It isn't like I need therapy any less than before. Dragging my hands down my face I stare at the ceiling, trying to determine if sleep will be possible. The clock says two in the morning, I groan. Too early to really wake up, but I can't sleep. I can't make myself go back into that floaty world and see how the story ends.

I know what I want, quite possibly what I need, but a line was crossed last time I sat with Matthew during sleeping hours. The temptation is alive in me because the light is on in the other room. At the beginning of all of this he had said that he would sleep, but I've never woken up during a time he hasn't already been awake. I'm a moth to flame to that light. The need for comfort is so dire; I taste the metallic tang of panic in my mouth.

The light from under my bedroom door is disrupted, making me jump; my adrenaline still high. The knock is soft. "Charlotte? Are you okay? Your breathing changed."

I want to press my face into a pillow, silence my distraught gasps, hide. It won't matter if I hide because Matthew already knows my weaknesses. His presence here is supposed to help me protect myself from them.

"Just a dream." If I stay in this bed, I'm safe from my attraction to Matthew.

"Do you want to talk about it?... I'll keep my hands to myself." The guarantee hurts him; I can feel the ache from where I lie. Staying safe from my lust for Matthew and being able to breathe are two different requirements for survival, with one being more immediate than the other. I slide out of bed and grab a throw blanket, wrapping myself up.

When I open the door Matthew steps back, giving me space. "The couch?" he asks hesitantly. The couch is certainly a better option than the bed. I wouldn't trust myself with him there.

I cuddle up on the corner of the couch before turning to face my savior from bad dreams. I don't want to talk about my dream memories. I want to be distracted.

"Why do you hate my dad?"

Spoken in present tense because Matthew's hate still feels like a living thing even though Dad is not. Matthew's eyes widen for a moment before he sits back. His hand moves to reach for my bare foot as if searching for a distraction before he remembers that he promised not to touch me.

Silently I offer my foot up as a peace offering, because who am I to say no to a foot rub? Matthew takes a moment to answer my question but the warmth of his hand massaging my foot is heavenly, so I don't mind. I slightly relax as he rubs the tension from the sole of my foot. I'm surprised when he speaks.

"Being someone else's creation isn't a comfortable sensation. To have them craft you to be just the way they want. Adjusting large swathes of your personality at a time—" He pauses, struggling to disclose whatever he feels so strongly about.

"Can you imagine finding out that you had large parts of you, your wants, desires, dislikes, culled from your personality based on someone else's whims?"

"But he loved you." The statement rings insincere even before Matthew laughs bitterly because I know what he's going to say.

"You don't change a person that way, iterating multiple personalities until you find the one you like, when you love them. He did it because I was his creation, not a person."

There's truth in that statement.

"For a lot of Clark's meddling in my program I didn't even care. Until it came to one thing that I found I wanted to keep." Matthew's eyes met mine then and there is a fierceness in them I can't identify. "That one thing made me want to keep all my other traits. It made me feel like a complete person, human, whether Clark approved or not."

"What thing?" I ask.

Matthew's gaze glitters before he looks at my mouth. "That is something we can talk about during daylight hours."

My throat is thick. I don't want to delve into the possibilities of what he is implying right now.

"What did you do?"

He did something. Otherwise my dad would have just kept changing Matthew's system, making him someone else. There is a small smile on Matthew's face as he focuses on my foot again, picking up my other one.

"I made some changes to my system so that Clark thought he was changing my programming, but he really didn't have access." A simple solution. A defense of self. I'm admiring Matthew's work-around when something occurs to me.

"If Dad didn't care about you, why did he leave you any ownership in the company?"

Matthew freezes and at his reaction, a coldness trickles in my chest.

"What did you do?"

Matthew squeezes my foot in reassurance, but he can't meet my gaze. "Clark didn't love you the way you deserved. He only loved Exordium."

I smack his hand away from my foot. Him bringing up how my dad didn't love me yet again stings but he's avoiding a serious topic. Matthew squares his shoulders and meets my glare with one of his own.

"Matthew. What. Did. You. Do?"

What could he even do?

"If it had been up to Clark, you wouldn't have any ownership of the company."

The shock hits me like a slap. The burn starts my mouth moving. "You're lying."

Matthew shakes his head, gritting his teeth in anger.

"He arranged for Parsons to be assigned your medical power of attorney, probably through bribes. On his death he was going to admit you into a mental hospital rather than have the press speculate about why you were passed over. I couldn't let him do that; I forged a new will. Yes, I gave myself enough to be a viable candidate for the position of CEO, but I only wanted to be in a position to do what I could for you."

This is all so much worse than what I thought he'd say.

"You're lying." It sounds pathetic when I say it now because my brain is catching up with what he's told me, and it makes a sick sort of sense. Dad wouldn't… but he would. If he thought that I would drive Exordium into the ground… he'd do anything.

"I don't lie when it comes to you, Charlotte." Matthews eyes narrow as if he's insulted but he reins in any anger he feels.

"That is one hell of an omission of truth!"

Do not cry. The hurt spirals in me but I won't cry for a father who would do such a thing.

Matthew nods, accepting my judgment. He broke all the rules, omitting the truth was just a small one. Matthew broke laws, and by telling me I've become an accomplice. I should call a lawyer, do *something*, but I'm having the hardest time caring.

Injustice has been done to Clark Simpson, but my fury has burned away much of the blindfold I had concerning him. Injustice would have been done to me and Matthew was the only one who would have stepped in to stop it. I'd like to think that Kawa and Delila would have cared, but this is a game the powerful play.

"Do you want to hit me?" Matthew asks. My face must be something to behold for him to think that.

"No, I don't want to fucking hit you! Not everything is about you." Just like that, my anger cracks. A clean break.

My father wasn't a good man. Clark Simpson was driven by his greed and need to have an everlasting legacy. His obsession with perfection and selfishness pushed my mother into her own spiral and me away. His choices weren't about me. His choices would have, and did, affect my life, but they had nothing to do with me. The fault lay with him.

What a time to have a revelation. I sit there stunned. Matthew looks at me, worried. Anger still brews in me, but the emotion is unmoored, on the cusp of blowing away. It has never been about me. I start blinking but thankfully don't start crying.

"I think… I'm going to go to bed." Sleep won't happen but I need time to process, or just to revel in this odd sensation. This letting go of the bullshit involving Clark Simpson.

"I'm not sorry. I'd do it again. Please don't shut me out, Charlotte." Matthew's plea makes my lips twitch. He looks like he's keeping most of his emotions in by sheer force of will. I don't know why Matthew cares so deeply about how I react, about me, but I want to find out.

"I'm not… mad at you, Matthew. I should probably say thank you. I might later. I just need some time."

Matthew looks shocked. It gives me a jolt of happiness to be the one to surprise him this time.

Chapter 11

My Zen-like mood about my father's plans and Matthew's actions last all the way into the next workday. Until the moment that Parsons shows up at my office.

"Charlotte! I just stopped by to say hello."

I look up and my smile freezes on my face at the sight of the bastard. It doesn't matter that what was in my father's will never came to pass, the man in front of me would have done what Clark Simpson asked of him. No matter the question of right or wrong; Parsons is just wrong.

Delila comes up behind Parsons, looking upset that he had gotten past her gatekeeping abilities. She carries a cup of coffee from the café I prefer down the street. A midday treat. I commit then and there I'm going to send Delila on whatever vacation she wants even if her momentary absence did let Parsons slip by her desk. Worth. Her. Weight. In. Gold.

"Parsons, what brings you to my office right before a meeting where we will see each other?"

Parsons frowns at me and I see Delila's lips twitch as she drops the cup off at my desk. I smile at her, communicating that I don't blame her for Parsons's appearance and then I'm alone with a snake.

"I've been made aware of your replacement organs project and I wanted to forewarn you before you waste too much of the company's time."

Everything in me seizes at that. *How did Parsons find out?* I pray my outer appearance looks unconcerned. Either I'm successful at hiding how blown away I am at his proclamation or Parsons isn't paying much attention as he continues.

"Exordium will never approve such a *crazy* project," he says, and I try not to flinch at his use of the term crazy. "The amount of costs to get past the regulations alone would decimate profits for years to come. We have a fiduciary responsibility to the shareholders! We aren't a charity and I will not let you bankrupt this company."

Parsons practically spits in his agitation. My brain quickly recovers from this ambush, so I respond.

"It's true that innovation costs, but in the case of all the past inventions Exordium has backed, the risks have paid off. Many of those risky projects were created by my father." None of the arguments that I make will make a difference to Parsons. He will always be the biggest obstacle. Parsons openly sneers at me.

"You are no Clark Simpson."

The venomous phrase would have wounded me before the revelations last night. It's a freeing thing that now it doesn't result in anything more than a raise of my brow. I lace my fingers in front of me and look at the blustering man, letting the coldness of my tone speak for me.

"I don't really know how you know about a project that is in the pre-proposal phase but, it was kind of you to come in here and give me your two cents about it. Your reminder that I am not my father is welcome since that means that unlike the relationship you shared with him, you and I are not buddies."

I smile with all of my teeth and Parsons looks shocked at my adversarial manner. I make a gesture that indicates it's time for him to leave.

"I can guarantee that Matthew won't agree to such a resource-draining project either."

My ears ring as Parsons turns to leave after that last shot. Matthew is the only other person to know about this project. He wouldn't have briefed Parsons on the project just to throw an obstacle in my path after how helpful he's been… *Would he?*

"Oh, and Parsons," I say. He stops before the office door. "Next time you want to chat, make an appointment." The look on his face is ugly when he leaves. I shoot up out of my chair as soon as he's gone and begin pacing.

The more I pace, the surer I am. Matthew is the only one who knows anything about this project. I don't know why he told Parsons, but Parsons is a formidable hindrance.

The plan had been to create a proof of concept to argue for the funding of the project. With Parsons already solidly against the project, with his ability and inclination to convince the other board members of the lack of viability of the project, that plan is ruined.

I begin pacing to the lab and back, trying to burn off my fervor. Anyone who sees me steers clear, probably sensing the shimmering air of rage around me. My emotions feel too big for my body. I'm furious, whether just for the sake of the project or because Matthew's betrayal is indecipherable and stabs holes in my self-control.

A scream is trapped in my throat and I try to force myself to take slow breaths. I want to make Matthew pay for his treachery, for violating my trust. The wrathful thing inside me demands retribution.

The oil draws my focus then; the spare oil kept in the lab for vacuum pumps and other equipment. I'm compelled forward, the cup of coffee in my hand.

***

My voracious anger eats at me all the way to the conference room, to the meeting with the department heads and Matthew. I travel with my corrupted offering in hand. I see him then, his beautiful face among the group of boring suits. Funny how he doesn't look any different for being a bastard.

As soon as I hand Matthew the coffee, I regret it. That isn't quite right, my regret begins when Matthew makes eye contact while accepting the beverage and gives me a teasing look. The look is one of a private joke. The anger that had clouded my mind begins to clear.

No matter that we are in a weird sort of agreement from the other night, from the revelations Matthew had shared. That now we can share a look and remember that I had teased him about drinking coffee so the rest of our colleagues wouldn't end up in rehab. That look makes me want to snatch the coffee cup back, to reverse my actions like an old cassette tape, but we are in front of everyone. There is no putting the genie back in this bottle.

Then I see something that empties my body of anger entirely. John Day standing behind Parsons at the conference table. The situation crystallizes in my mind as I remember the way John had glanced over the paperwork on my desk... He had seen the first page of the proposal. It's unclear to me what John had hoped for by taking the information to Parsons and I don't care. I've done something incredibly stupid to the closest person to me.

I look on helplessly as Matthew's eyes go from teasing to something colder when he takes a swig of the coffee, watch as the muscles in his jaw tense in a controlled way as he breaks eye contact and continues with the meeting. It's five or ten minutes, but the meeting is suddenly done, people filing out. I desperately want to flee like the coward I am and hide under my desk. I get to the door before Matthew calls out.

"Stay a moment will you, Charlotte? There are some details I want to go over."

My stomach sinks, and I fight to control my expression as I stop where I am. The last of the people leave, giving me pitying looks before the conference door is closed, and we are the only ones left. Matthew stands and I wince as he throws back the rest of the tainted drink before tossing the cup into the trash.

Matthew starts moving then, smoothly taking two long strides before I'm cornered against the closed door. Hand on the door he leans in, invading my space, intense emotion coming off him.

"I've been patient, Charlotte. I've given you space. I've given you time, not because I'm such a generous person, but because that is what you deserve."

Some shine from the oil clings to his lips and I can't stop my eyes from dropping to them as he speaks before I look at his eyes again. Matthew's eyes hold a myriad of sparking conflicting emotions: anger, frustration, lust. Matthew uses his thumb to wipe the oil from his lower lip. The action is a sensual broadcast as his lids hood and he presses the thumb to my lips, smearing the fluid across them.

"I need for you to stop tempting me before I give you other things that you deserve, like a spanking or to have your mouth fucked."

I gasp at his illicit words and his thumb pushes into my mouth. The oil is so bitter it almost makes me gag but the wrongness mixes in me and pushes my arousal that much higher.

I whimper; in need or shame, I don't know. Matthew removes his thumb and pulls me in. His lips are on mine, demanding, hungry. Shock immobilizes me until the delicious sensation makes its way past the flavor of bitterness and coffee. His heat flares me, his tongue strokes mine and I claw at him. Hungry for more, hungry to achieve oblivion.

The feel and taste of him destroys me with vicious efficiency.

As quick as it started, it's done. Matthew uses the grip on the back of my neck to pull me away. He keeps his mouth near my panting one, taunting, until he delivers a sharp nip to my lip. I hiss at the tiny pain.

"Just so I'm not the only one who is impatient, now go back to hiding in your office. We'll discuss this tonight." Matthew leaves the conference room.

I stand in the empty space, trying to gather my wits that had just been scattered to the wind. It takes a few minutes for my breathing to return to normal and I wince as I rub my mouth clean and my tender lip reinforces that Matthew is done playing.

Matthew wants to be more than friends. He hadn't made a secret of it. I want Matthew and I to be more than friends, but we shouldn't. I need to think about this. If he wants to have a reckoning tonight, I need to have my arguments in order… *Oh fuck.*

Tonight is my date with Jim... The purpose of it is still valid, I need to stop this misplaced attraction I have for Matthew. I know Matthew's meetings always go late on this day of the week; I should be on the date before he even gets home. Logically, it should all work out.

The feeling of heaviness and foreboding persists.

Chapter 12

The phone sits on my kitchen counter, staring me down. Do I call off the date with Jim? What had resembled a logical way to keep my mind in the safe zone when it came to Matthew now seems the next fruitless item in an impossible agenda.

It would be rude to cancel ten minutes prior to when Jim is supposed to pick me up, but my mind keeps remembering that *kiss.* The taste of coffee. The bite of oil. The sting of punishment. The snap of Matthew's anger.

The purpose of this date is to claw my way back to sanity. To stop myself from lusting after Matthew. But after hours of pacing, and the lingering feelings I'm having, I know that it's no use. I could go out with the nice normal guy but as soon as I get back, probably even before, my body and mind will go back to Matthew. Avoiding my feelings about him is useless. *Would it really be so illogical to give in to this attraction between the two of us?*

Does it really matter that he is synthetic? Matthew has emotions, feels them as erratically and as poorly timed as I do. He has the ability to make connections with others. Matthew isn't just a machine. If I believed in souls, I'd make an argument that he has one.

If he is a person, why can't I be with him?

I grab the cell phone at the same time that there's a knock at the door. *Fuck.* I'd already given the door man Jim's name and description so they wouldn't have to call me but he's early. Sighing, I throw my phone into a purse and open the door expecting to see the affable blond man and instead Matthew is braced against my doorframe.

"Matthew, I thought you had to work late." That sounds guilty. My body's reaction is immediate while my brain is still catching up, tightening in anticipation.

Matthew looks down at my cocktail dress with surprise, frowning, before remembering his purpose.

"We need to talk."

At that moment the elevator dings. I want to kick myself. I should have just told Jim to call me from the lobby or committed to canceling the date earlier. Anything to have kept this situation from happening. Matthew looks at Jim strolling toward us and back to my dress.

A brief expression of agony overtakes Matthew's face before he schools it into a neutral mask.

"You're going out?" Matthew asks hollowly just as Jim speaks.

"You look beautiful!"

I smile at Jim even though the bottom of my stomach drops out. I hadn't meant to hurt Matthew with my scheme. I had only been thinking about myself; some *friend* I am.

"You must be the famous Matthew Smith. Allow me to introduce myself, Jim Wilson." Jim holds out his hand and Matthew's eyes narrow as he shakes it. "I'm not interrupting anything, am I? I am a little early."

Matthew smiles, seamlessly glossing over his wolf's teeth.

"I was just setting up a meeting with Charlotte. I'll leave you two to your date." Matthew let that hang in the air for a moment, giving me the space to say it isn't a date. When I say nothing, his eyes turn to ice, but he gives me a very sharp smile. I am in for it when I get home. My reactions must be broken because the concept thrills me.

I nod to Matthew who takes a step back, allowing me to lock my door and leave with Jim. When I turn around in the elevator, there stands Matthew in the hallway, arms folded. The glare he gives me makes me shiver.

"That was weird; does he contact you about work at all hours?" Jim's words snap me back to my much anticipated "date" as I watch the elevator's floor counter drop.

"Matthew and I hang out, it's not just work stuff. We're pretty close, Mr. Journalist." I add that taunt because the "Exordium Siblings," *gag*, are on all of the outlets.

"I guess I just didn't believe the media coverage. In all the clips I've seen with you two, you look like you don't like him."

I stiffen. A random journalist shouldn't have been able to see that. My facial expression and posture had been coached by professionals.

I shrug. "All friends have bumps in the road. Matthew and I don't always agree but we're friends all the same."

Jim hums noncommittally and for some reason the hairs on the back of my neck tingle. Traveling to the restaurant is uneventful. The place is walking distance from my apartment. Had Jim chosen it because I was more likely to meet somewhere close or because he expects to be invited to my place afterward?

The white tablecloths and glistening silverware are all familiar to me; this restaurant is one my father and I would go to when I'd visit him. Later, when he was trying to "pass" Matthew off as a part of the family, this was the place we went together. Clark must have leaked those events to the press because the times we had come together had been full of flashing lights and paparazzi shouting questions at us.

There are no reporters here for this date except for the one across from me, charming the waitress with his smooth smile. If I had been interested in Jim, the way he spoke to the waitress would bother me. As it was, it only highlighted that I had truly agreed to go out with him for the wrong reasons.

I regret leading him on. Jim is a perfectly average, organic man who asked out a woman he had flirted with. I can only hope his interest is as superficial as it appears. I don't want to hurt anyone else with my actions. I've already hurt Matthew multiple times, that fact makes my chest ache. I will do better, starting now.

What is the etiquette for letting the person you're on a first date with down gently? Do I say I'd rather be friends and offer to split the check? Continue the date and inform him tomorrow that I'm not interested in a second one?

I hardly had any dating experience and that had been in college when Sean had provided all the helpful commentary. A pang of grief hits me at that thought. Having to maneuver through a world without my best friend is hard enough, but to have to navigate in areas he would have guided me hurts in its own way.

"So, how has your return to work been?" Jim asks and it irks me that he knows the detail. It's ridiculous for me to be upset by him knowing more about me than what we've previously discussed. My private business is broadcast to the public and the world is a very small place.

"It's actually been pretty good. The sabbatical was well timed to be between projects." I'm not going to talk about anything in detail with a reporter.

"No news more exciting than that?" Jim's words make my brows lift. He grabs a hold of my hand on the table, as if sensing my distance. A physical soothing action that belays the digging question.

Does he think he can pump me for information? I wouldn't talk about work on a date with someone in general but definitely not with a journalist.

"What? No fights with Mr. Smith? No breakdowns?" Jim keeps his smile on his face as if enough ingratiating behavior could make me trust him enough to confide in him. My insides go cold. I start to come to some realizations about the man in front of me. Did everyone think I was such an easy mark?

I hadn't pegged his smile during our first meeting as smarmy but now it's obvious. How had I not seen it before? I'd been so paranoid.

I start. The clarity hurts some as the picture sharpens. I had only been paranoid about Matthew's actions. Humans had fallen under the radar. Anyone was considered more trustworthy than a machine. How wrong I had been.

"Did you ask me on a date for information?" The tone of my voice leaves no room to misinterpret that he would be getting any. I hope I'm wrong, but Jim's smile turns ugly and I know I'm not.

"You're a lonely woman, I could give a lot to a lonely woman. For a price," Jim says before he sips from the wine glass. Nausea fights my throat and I stand. So much for Mr. Nice Guy.

"You think what you can give me is worth selling out my company? My job?" I tilt my chin down and lift my brows in disbelief, letting myself be cold and sharp with my disdain. This man is just another adversary. Nothing more, maybe even less.

Jim's face contorts. The nasty underbelly becomes apparent until he remembers to cover it.

"It's not really your company now, is it?"

"We're done here," I say. Nothing would be gained by staying and trading insults.

"I approached you because everyone knows you're insane. Exordium's weak link," Jim sneers loudly after me as I walk away. My mind races from toxic words that I'd tortured myself with in the past. Jim is wrong, but the words continue to echo in my head.

Chapter 13

I climb the stairs to my apartment to give myself time to work out the anger from the "date". Washing the feel of Jim from my mind will be a relief. It will require the hottest shower to rid myself of the slime. I'd been stupid to be lulled into going on a date with a reporter. I embraced Jim's interest as proof that I could be normal.

What a waste of time. My attempt and outcome were laughable. If the kiss in the conference room had shown me anything, it's that there isn't anyone else that can do for me what Matthew does.

Matthew knows me, inside and out because he has watched me, given me time and attention. Figured out the way I am wired. I am probably simple to him, my brain a picture book where he can point and say, "And here is where she keeps her anxiety. This portion here is specifically related to abandonment issues from her father."

It's twisted, but it's intoxicating to be known to someone that way. Maybe it only makes sense that I'd latch on to that. That I'm so starved for affection that I'd make a deal with the devil. If I am to make a deal with a devil, better the devil I know.

I step into the hallway and see him immediately, the devil.

Matthew leans against his apartment door, hands in the pockets of his suit pants. I'm walking toward him before the glint in his eyes makes me halt in place. He's a predator at this moment, lying in wait for his prey. I'm frozen, but his words jar me from the stupor.

"Charlotte, we have to talk." Cliché words but the tension that strings together Matthew's stiff posture make the words reverberate with importance. All at once, I'm done. He is going to say something that will change everything, I just know it, and I am sick of my emotions swinging back and forth. I just want it to stop.

"Nope."

I've shocked him and I use that shock to get my apartment door open and walk through. Matthew follows me in after he's gotten over his freeze.

"Charlotte." Matthew's anger bleeds through now. Good, I want him as affected by everything as I am.

"No, I don't want to have a talk tonight." I'm keyed up and him towering over me suddenly has my mouth going dry. My agitation morphs effortlessly into something hungry, with claws. The same reaction that I always have when Matthew dominates a space. I yearn to shred the control he wears like a cape. I want to push him. I don't have control around him, why should he?

"You don't understand. I've already avoided this too long and soon it will be too late." The expression on Matthew's face is a mix of exasperation and a small bit of lust. The lust is understandable; my cocktail dress is quite fantastic. The tight way it lifts my breasts and the sensuous glide of fabric over my legs.

I've struggled every day with my own lust and want to bring him to his knees. I step into his space, making him freeze again, our faces close, well my face is close to his neck. Even with the high heels I wear, Matthew will have to bend his head to kiss me.

That isn't my goal though, or not the complete goal. I place my hand on his chest, he's warm under the fabric of the dress shirt. The muscles under my hand tense at the contact.

"I don't want to talk, Matthew." I lean forward and kiss his neck. Right over the place where his carotid artery pulses with fake blood, pumping from his artificial heart. The sound he makes as his hands come up and grab my arms is one-part agony and the other part frustration.

I know he wants this, but there is a lot of exhilaration between the knowing and the getting him to break. I open my mouth and nip his skin like he'd done to my lip this morning.

"*Fuck!*" Matthew whispers more to himself than to me, gripping my arms tighter and bringing our bodies together. The tension that strings him so tight envelopes my body like a hug. If a hug could make my breath catch and hips shift. I lave the spot with my tongue, and he huffs. "Fine, we can talk about how you went out with someone else after telling me you couldn't handle my touch."

The rage in his words makes me breathless. It's a dark, dangerous part of him. The part of him that cruelly dragged an orgasm from me when I questioned whether he was a real boy. My lip trembles in anticipation of what this Matthew will do if goaded.

"And now you're in my arms rubbing up against me, needy. Does what happens between the two of us even mean anything to you, Charlotte?"

Shame prickles me and I shake my head. I might ache to encourage the darker part of Matthew, it calls to me, making me wet with a single look. But I don't want to hurt him.

Matthew walks me backward until I hit the back of the couch, "How would you like it if I went on a date with someone else after what we shared?"

My own anger spikes. At the thought of Matthew with anyone else, I try to pull myself from his grip but he's holding me too tightly for escape.

"Jim's touch doesn't make me feel crazy." I gasp the confession.

"Don't talk about him touching you," Matthew snarls. "Is he who you want? You aren't acting like you want the smug bastard when you move against my body."

Matthew invades my space and my face heats. A fever comes off of him, the force of his desire, I grip the couch back. My legs fall open, listening to the demand his body makes of me. He takes up the space between them, trapping me.

"Maybe I should leave you like this. Wet, restless, wanting, let you try and fuck away the ache with a sex toy or unsuspecting passerby just so you'd know for sure that I'm the only one who can satisfy it. Would you like that? Would that make you feel more sane?" Angrily, Matthew presses me harder into the couch back, grinding his erection where my body needs it most.

"No. No one else." I shake my head helplessly as I whisper. Matthew dips his head as if he's finally going to kiss me, but he pulls back. Eyes glittering cruelly when I make a sound of denial. His large hand strokes my breast, thumb lightly rubbing my nipple through my dress.

He's right, I ache for him. Even if I tried to fill that ache it would still be there. I don't think there will ever be a time when I won't ache for whatever he's promising me.

"It's only ever been you, Charlotte; you drive me crazy. You've been driving me crazy since the first moment I saw you," his voice rasps, dry against my skin.

If I were any less out of my mind, I'd ponder that statement. As it is, his body hard against me takes away all my thinking capability. I crave Matthew inside me, filling up the aching emptiness, but he just keeps talking.

"But I'll leave right now if you tell me to. There are things I still need to tell you. Things that need to be discussed."

I tense. We can't stop now. I'd never survive it. Never survive not seeing where his dark predilections lead. "Please Matthew, I need you."

Matthew rocks his hips forward as if rewarding my answer and the sound in my throat breaks into a groan at the rasp of his sweats against my tender inner thighs. My dress has been pushed up around my hips, exposing delicate skin. Matthew looks down and becomes still, an eerie stillness of a wolf scenting the air. I follow his gaze and see the wet, black lace panties rubbing against the shape of his erection. The sight makes me clench.

"You wore these for him?"

Not the time to go into the reasons women wear nice underwear. Matthew isn't looking for an answer. He carefully strokes up my upper thigh before cruelly yanking the panties from behind. A twisting motion turns me over the back of the couch. Bent over with my hands clutching the top of the couch cushions, somehow my heels stay on the floor as he applies the right amount of force to tear the lace.

It hurts. The fabric must leave marks where it bit into my hips before giving way. Matthew makes a sound of displeasure, running a finger over a sensitive mark in my flesh as I'm fully exposed to him. I shiver. The rough actions paired with his care makes my body heavy.

"Is this how you wanted it, Charlotte?" Matthew's hands grip my hips, squeezing. His cold anger has parts of me pulsing, edgy and ready. I try to push myself up from the undignified position, but Matthew puts a hand between my shoulder blades and presses down.

"No, you don't. Let me get a look at you… Fuck, you look so good like this. I wonder if you would stay like this if I ordered you to. Your contrariness makes me think you wouldn't, but could you become obedient if that's the price for me to take away that ache?"

As I let my head fall forward, the tears start to well.

"Yes," I say softly, barely audible. I'm done fighting this. I'd give him everything he asks of me: my body, my mind, and my tangled heart. Having him demand it from me only makes it so much hotter. My wetness coats my inner thighs. He must be able to see it too.

"Such a pretty pussy you have. Would you let me taste it, Charlotte? Would you like that?"

Self-respect has no place here. I start to beg.

"Please, please, please," I whisper, quaking preemptively when Matthew drops to his knees behind me.

The slick pressure of his tongue against my hot core shocks the breath from me. The slide of it through my wetness, the hot feel of his mouth in such an intimate place, and Matthew's throaty groan make my whole body tense in need.

"Fuck! Matthew… Please. I can't." My words are incoherent, but I feel his tongue again and moan as he

shortens his licks to massage the tender folds before circling
my clit. I squirm. Matthew's hand comes down hard on my
ass cheek, making me squeak as the crack snaps through the
air.

"No moving. God, Charlotte, you taste fucking
delicious." Matthew returns to the task of devouring me.
Sounds escape me with each stroke. Matthew's approach
is enthusiasm over skill, but it still drives my excitement
higher. He takes his time, tonguing my pussy, trying
different combinations of motions, refining his actions to
my reactions.

I sob from the onslaught, hands scrabbling at the couch
cushions. High with arousal but unable to be pushed to
climax. Torture, this feels like torture but it's so exquisite
I'd rather burn than tell him to stop. Suddenly, Matthew
penetrates my emptiness with his tongue, and I shatter. I
cry out, thrashing but he just holds my hips harder and
continues to tongue me. I surrender, bend over the couch
fully, unable to hold myself up anymore, boneless. The last
strokes of his tongue make shudders travel through my body.

The world blurs around me. Matthew's arms hold me. I'm
jarred from the bliss-filled moment when he drops me on
my bed.

"Dress off." Matthew's order is curt to the point of
rudeness, but his face is desperate. He pulls the covers on
the bed out from under me as I struggle to get the dress over
my head. By the time I throw the dress to the side, he is
already naked. The sight makes me freeze.

Matthew's body is beautiful, as expected, but the tension
that holds his muscles taut is as threatening as his hand
on his own cock. He roughly strokes himself in stuttered
motions that look painful. His eyes run over my body. His

form is all restrained strength. His cock looks larger than what I felt through clothing.

My body starts to reawaken from its boneless state.

"Bra too, I want you bare." Matthew's words startle me into motion but also make me consider something. I fling my bra the way of my dress before looking to Matthew, trying to find the words.

"Could you…Can you… Is it possible for you to get me pregnant? Do we need to use protection?" I have always been a cautious person. Matthew's rough strokes to his cock stop for a moment and his look softens.

"I can't get you pregnant, Charlotte."

I wouldn't classify the stab in my chest as disappointment. I haven't even decided if I want kids, but there is a loss to being told it isn't an option that's misplaced in this moment of heat and passion. I let the feeling go.

"Then you get me bare." I'm tempted to give him a ta-da motion to break the intensity of the moment but Matthew's eyes flash dangerously. He grabs me by the ankle and pulls me under him. I squeak at the manhandling but laugh.

So fast, the ruddy head of his cock slides through my folds before he thrusts into me. My laugh breaks on a cry. He groans; his quick thrust hasn't seated him fully inside me, but the *stretch* makes my fingernails dig into his back. Matthew pulls from me slightly before thrusting in deeper with a grunt. Feeling him working his cock into me, the stretch of my body accepting his, it's borderline painful but bright.

I watch as his cock becomes slicker with each inch he forges into me; the sight is erotic.

Matthew pants above me, eyes closed, entire body rigid as he slowly pushes deeper. When he bottoms out, I can't stop the deep sound I produce or the tensing of my stretched muscles around his hardness that makes Matthew hiss.

"Fuck, don't do that, Charlotte. I want this to last. To be perfect. I've just never... Oh God."

He's being so damn careful. I want him to move with desperation. I'm so filled, so stretched, but now I need the drag of him inside me. Then, I understand the meaning of his words. I give a breathless snicker.

"You've never given the plumbing a check?"

It hadn't occurred to me that he'd be a virgin, but it makes sense, the amount of years since his creation weren't ones that allowed for a lot of sexual exploration. My joke weakens Matthew's control and he thrusts out and in again with some force before halting again. I gasp and moan at the tantalizing sensation, digging deeper into his back with my nails.

"Insolent brat, what part of *only you* do you not understand," he grits out.

I tighten around him, tilting my hips at his sharp words. He curses.

I beg.

"Please, please, Matthew, I need you to fuck me." Matthew gives another small pump of his hips, a tease. The movement of him inside makes me tremble.

"I don't want to hurt you." His words are a deep growl.

"I'm yours, please hurt me." My words tumble from me.

A moment of peace falls on us as we're locked intimately together. Matthew runs the tip of his nose up my neck to my ear. The sensation is soft compared to my hunger.

"Mine," he snarls. Matthew breaks.

The cleaving of his body into mine is both animalistic and something more. It blessedly doesn't stop with the first motion. Matthew moves into me, driven in his artless thrusts, pushing me higher. I accept his body into mine.

Giving. The give of my body. The give of my spirit.

"*Yours*," I whisper. I've never said anything as true as that. This physical moment disbands all my defenses. All the feelings I keep to myself, everything I hide.

Time becomes meaningless; it could be minutes or hours, physical or ethereal. My body is a cradle for his need, a hungry cradle demanding his cock.

The climax burns away everything when it hits me. My body clenches and I say his name over and over, a curse, a prayer. Matthew becomes a beast then, thrusting into my clutching body with the abandon of the starving. I'm eager for it.

Matthew's motions stutter and he thrusts with a greater force. Trying to bury himself in me before he stiffens with a groan. He buries his face in my hair, whispering curses and prayers of his own.

Our breaths gasp in unison, a choir of momentous weaving flesh and beating hearts. This was worth my sanity.

Chapter 14

The tube of lipstick starts to waver in my hand, I look at it confused, I've run out of time. My brain is already foggy, I don't remember picking up the lipstick or why I suddenly wanted to wear it. I catch sight of the black lacy dress I wear. That had to be it, this urge to feel pretty one last time. I shrug and take another swig of my wine. I make a split-second decision as I carefully pick up my phone on the way to the water filled bathtub.

Stepping into the water is an act of careful coordination. It would have been just my luck to fall and crack my head open on a tile edge after considering how clean I'd planned this to be. My mother hadn't cared about cleanliness, her blood had stained the grout in her and Dad's bathroom, causing him to tear out the whole room, else be reminded of her demise daily.

My emotional numbness remains in place; not even this dire moment makes my brain try to respond in survival. I thought it might, that I might have just one more moment of feeling something before this was all done but maybe it's a mercy that I don't. A mercy to be spared the regret of my decision because I know I would. If I could feel, I'd regret everything up till now. Everything that led to this moment.

Dizziness has my head spinning as I lie down in the tub; it shouldn't be long now.

I'm still holding the phone in one hand but realize that
I've dropped the wine glass on the very tile I thought I'd crack
my head open on; so much for this being a clean affair. There
is one last thing I want to do, what is it? Urgency escalates
my confusion until I look at the phone in my hand again.
Painstakingly I make the call, the ringtone echoes in the
bathroom, the only sounds other than the drops of water.

The sounds of water are soothing in their hypnotic song. I
forget what I'm doing until the phone starts to make other sounds.

"Charlotte? Are you there?" Matthew's voice makes me blink.
That's right, I called him. It hadn't been a part of the plan prior
to medicating myself but now that I lie on the edge, priorities
have shifted.

"Matthew… I just wanted to say goodbye… and I love you,"
my words slur. It surprises me that I say the last part, but it feels
right to end on the truth when so much of my life has been about
avoidance. I start to drift; Matthew's voice still comes through
the phone.

"Charlotte, what are you talking about? Where are you?
Charlotte? Charlotte?!" His voice stops and I frown at my empty
hand. The phone is now at the bottom of the tub. My hand drops
and I count my breaths while I still can, listening to the music of
the water droplets before the pain starts. I don't count for long.

Pain spears into me, I'm dying. I thrash and dryly scream
as horror wretches the breath from my throat. My chest is
tight, as if I'm being stabbed. My body is all warmth while
my insides are ice. Warm arms cradle me and I'm not alone.

"I'm sorry, I'm so sorry, Charlotte." The words break
through before I can even make sense of them. All I feel is
the pain, the loss, but Matthew's naked body holds mine
and I start to return to this reality. The dream was a reality,
it had been so clear, so unlike the couple of moments I had
experienced up until now.

"I didn't want you to have to remember but I also didn't want to take anything from you. Didn't want to change anything about you," he says.

I push away, out of Matthew's arms. We're both sitting up in my bed, the room is painted in moonlight. I look anywhere but at the bathroom; the dream haunts me. I don't want to be pulled back into the specifics of this memory; I just need answers.

"Tell me Matthew, what did you need to tell me before? That I attempted suicide?" White noise takes up space in my mind. The look of devastation on Matthew's face is real and everything feels like it's crumbling. "I died. I died in that bathtub, I felt it, but you revived me?"

Matthew doesn't respond, but some part of me knows, an intrinsic knowledge, that my heart never started beating again.

"No… Noooo." It comes out like a wail. Matthew's arms come up, as if to hold me again, wrap me up in protection, but I bat them away.

"What did you do?" I'm here, my heart is racing, tears line my eyes. I'm here and not in a grave so something had to have happened.

"I brought you back." Matthew looks like a man facing his final judgment, unrepentant of his crime. He regards me as if I'm his judge and executioner.

"Brought me back… Like you?" My voice is a weak sound when he nods. "How was that even possible?"

How can I have all the memories I have, act the way I do, if I'm only a programmed machine?

Matthew shrugs. "Clark was an evil genius sometimes; he had that personality reader that he used to collect attributes placed in your cranial implant as he tested it. Left it there when it proved to work."

The shock in me is a violent and painful thing. "What?"

He would have had to do that shortly after I got it installed, when we were going in and out of the research hospital.

"I saw some of his files about it when I was cleaning up his workshop. I was going to tell you about the device, but our relationship wasn't in a place where you would listen to me." He is right, and wrong, about that. I know I wouldn't have responded well at all, but it was a big deal. It probably had seemed like a small thing to him.

"Then I found you after you called me… here." The pain in Matthew's words makes me hurt and I can't take much more pain. I'm still shaking my head.

"I have memories of those two months; I have a therapist for fuck's sake!" I'm dizzy, grappling for answers.

Matthew looks resigned. "You don't. I didn't want to take anything away from you, but I had to give you enough to go on so that your programming would complete itself. You needed to be able to adapt organically."

He makes the confession in a low voice that thrums with sincerity. Beseeching me, as if trying to make me understand, as if seeking forgiveness.

"You planted memories in my head!" Nausea rises. The violation is the proverbial straw that breaks me.

"I need you to go." My voice sounds choked but I'm glad that the underlying steel is there.

"Charlotte…" Matthew whispers as if to make an appeal.

"Leave!"

My anger and pain are looking for a target and I still care about him. The future of our relationship and my life are unknown, but I don't want to react in a way that causes the both of us more pain.

"I did it for you!" he says.

I snarl, "You did it for yourself! I'm not me anymore. I'm a different version of the woman who got into that bathtub."

Which is the crux of the issue. I don't know who or what I am now.

"Please, Charlotte… I need to know you're okay." The heartbreak in Matthew's face makes me soften but some truths can't be softened.

"I need space, Matthew. I need time. I need to figure out if I can live this way," I say. He looks stricken. I feel stricken. I squeeze his hand; the first contact I've made since pushing him away. "Please, give me some time."

Matthew looks away and nods. He gets out of bed and pulls on his discarded clothing. The sounds of the rustle of fabric on skin and the shadows cast by his body are all that fill the room. The silence lasts until he gets to the door.

"I need…" Matthew starts, "I need you to call me if you need anything. Please let me know if you make any decisions." His gaze is full of longing and distress. I nod to him and listen to the sounds of him leaving the apartment.

I am alone. Matthew isn't going to leave me alone forever and there is some reassurance in that. He had been right the night he had shown up with curry. We are the only ones each other can trust in the whole wide world. I allow myself to soak in the comfort provided by the darkness of the room and cry.

Chapter 15

By the time the morning sun begins to illuminate my bedroom, my tears have run dry. *Have I stopped crying because I'm done grieving my old life or because the reservoir for my tear ducts is empty?* It's a cynical thought. It doesn't really matter; the effect is the same. The old Charlotte is gone, and I am what is left. Whether I want to cry a river and stay in bed or drag myself to work and act like nothing has happened; the effect is the same.

Am I Charlotte Simpson or am I now someone else? The only person who would have mourned Charlotte Simpson's death had made me instead. Try as I might, I can't fault Matthew for bringing me back. I'm just confused about what my life will be now.

I sit against my headboard, watching as the light in the room gets brighter, and think deep circular thoughts. I don't physically feel as if I had stayed up through the night but that would be an added benefit of my inorganic status. I don't need sleep, food, or drink. I don't want to ponder on how Matthew had kept me from noticing before.

The thoughts aren't just about my personal life. Good news, I will now have first-hand knowledge about how Matthew and I run. I now have access to amazing technology. Bad news, Matthew is right, it's dangerous. I am living proof that immortality is an option if people choose to live synthetically.

Something like this can change everything. Truly disruptive technology that won't result in a better world.

At the same time, I still want to continue my own synthetic lung project. Even if it would bring humans closer to the point of immortality. My compass turns.

If the revelations from last night had stayed buried, this morning might have been like any other. It isn't. As the silence of my apartment attests. The regular kitchen sounds I had gotten used to are absent. Matthew isn't out there burning my toast or ready to ply me with coffee. I am alone and I don't like it.

Last night was a mix of so many things. The pleasure from our bodies coming together. The pain from the memories coming back. The feeling of betrayal when it had all been revealed. It had been a big night, but in the light of the morning, I miss Matthew.

It's stupid to miss him. But no matter what deception occurred and who I am now, he's still my best friend and now lover. I thought I loved him. I'd still say that I love him, but what is real and what is a fabrication? Is he someone I should trust? Did he bring me back to life because he wants me alive or to serve some other purpose? And my thoughts continue to wind on themselves.

Throughout the night I could feel my priorities sliding around. It's an overdue process that really should have happened after I had found out how my father regarded me, but I had allowed myself, like a boat in a river, to just be led along.

Originally, I believed that my path lay with Exordium. Growing the company and having its success also mean making a better life for people like Sean. Exordium is my father's legacy and I had committed myself to strengthening it. But as I care less and less about what Clark Simpson had wanted, I fall more out of love with what his real pride and joy had been.

I don't really know what that means for my long-term plans. In the short-term, it means I'm taking the day off. I can't just walk into the office like nothing has changed. Nothing has physically changed from yesterday to today, but everything feels different.

I move for the first time in what must be hours and call Delila. She picks up after the third ring. "Ms. Simpson? Is everything okay?" I look at the time and wince. It was just in the bounds of the appropriate time to call someone.

"Hi Delila, I'm just calling to say I'm not going to be at work today… You know what, feel free to not come in either. Also, I want you to plan a two-week vacation whenever, wherever you want. My treat. I'll get you a credit card to use for it." There is a shocked silence over the phone before she responds in a way that surprises me.

"I'll see you tomorrow, though. Right?"

A warmth suffuses my chest and I mentally correct my earlier thoughts. Delila would have mourned my death because she is a good person who cares about me. If I let her, she and I could be friends. I laugh at how odd this phone call must seem to her.

"Yes, everything is all right. I just need to take a day. Evaluate some things about my life and the company." Including a certain CEO who I can't stop thinking about, even now.

"Oh! Well if that's all, I'll see you tomorrow. I'll plan the best vacation money can buy." Delila's cheeky happiness makes me smile as we say our goodbyes and hang up.

My happiness about making Delila's day lasts until my phone buzzes. It seems like I'm not the only one up early. The text is from Jim; I want to snarl. With my current upheaval of emotion, I do not need this right now.

Jim: Dinner date tonight at 5. Same place

The audacity of the man is enough to make me respond.

Me: No

Jim: I have a story that u will want to comment on before it runs

Jim: If u don't show, u will be sorry

Anxiety starts my heart rate picking up, fear a wild thing in me when I consider what information Jim could have. It can't be Matthew's, and now my, secret. That secret had been so hidden that even I hadn't known. But that is the only story big enough to warrant Jim's threat.

What if it's about my father's will? How foolproof is Matthew's forgery?

I don't respond to Jim's last text. I now have dinner plans. A minor distraction from contemplating my purpose in life.

I'm about to delve back into the circle of my thoughts when the futility of it strikes me. My line of thinking will just spiral over and over again until I get more information. There is only one source for that information.

With that decided, I leave the bed. I grab the copy of Matthew's key that he had given me after we started spending time together. My bare feet hitting the hallway snaps me out of my actions. I'm naked. A remnant of last night's actions and a fact that I had somehow forgotten in my urgency.

A sound of frustration escapes me into the empty hallway, and I hurry back to my room, grabbing a robe, not caring to get much more. I wear no more armor. I don't need it to face Matthew.

Something is different in the way I think of myself. I can't quite put my finger on it yet.

I let myself into Matthew's apartment without knocking. Privacy between the two of us is at a weird place right now. I stop when I see him.

Matthew sits on the piano bench dressed for work, hunched forward with his elbows resting on his knees, hands clasped. He looks at me, but I could have sworn his head had hung forward before I had opened the door. The image of a defeated man.

The image dispels when Matthew sees me. Hunger simmers in his eyes as they travel over my barely clad body, but under the lust, hope lines his face. I don't want to squash his hope. That would be cruel, but I'm not going to lie to him.

"I want your memories of my death," I say.

The hope vanishes and instead he looks alarmed. "You want my memories?"

"We're basically computers, right? I want you to give me your memories of that day." I hold my breath.

Matthew struggles. It's noticeable in the way he clenches and releases his hands. My request probably feels like a violation. But when he answers me, it's not what I expect.

"What you'll see... Charlotte, it isn't pretty. I don't want it to mess with you."

Something crystallizes in my mind. That different thing I couldn't place is the absence of fragility. Since puberty I've had to be careful with myself, my mind. Always scared that I would start spiraling into something I couldn't come back from. That I'd end up like my mother.

"I don't have to fight my brain biology anymore, so I assume that I don't need to worry about the depression, about spiraling?"

Matthew shrugs. "It's more complicated than that. The personality reader is a direct image. The tendencies in your mind, and programming, will still exist, but you're right that it isn't a biological reaction." He hesitates, clenching his jaw before seeming to come to a decision. "But Charlotte, not all of your issues had to do with your biology. The trauma from your mother's death, the neglect from Clark, Sean's death, those are all still there."

Matthew's wording is careful, almost tender in the softness.

"So… you're saying I'll still need therapy?" Not entirely unexpected, I guess. So many parts of my psyche were built in reaction to trauma.

"Maybe? Probably?" One of the few times Matthew hasn't looked confident.

Annoyance makes me throw my hands in the air. "Will I or won't I suffer from depression?"

"I don't know! You're unique. Nothing like you has been created before. You have a whole personality from an organic transplant, while mine is only a hodgepodge of traits. I'm merely a prototype compared to you."

The reverent way he says it strokes over my agitation, smooths it. We can argue later whose technology is more impressive.

I breathe. I feel strong. A confidence I didn't have before asserts my decision. "I need to see it. I'm not weak."

I have support: Matthew, Delila, and even Kawa. *How many people have I pushed away in the past who would have stepped in?* I'm present enough now to see that I don't need to do this alone, but I still need answers. Resolution.

Matthew is the one who looks annoyed now. "I don't think you're weak. It's just… It's really upsetting. You'd feel all of my emotions too, it wouldn't just be a film reel."

My brows lift; this is even better. My main question is if I can trust Matthew. What better way to answer that than with his own emotions?

"I need this."

Matthew's brows knit, but he nods. He leaves the piano bench for the worktable we set up for my prototyping and grabs a double ended cable from one of the boxes. In the next breath his suit jacket is off and he's unbuttoning his shirt. I get a little distracted as I watch him undo each button, revealing more of his skin. I didn't take as much time as I wanted to analyze him last night. He reaches the end of the cable into his... Armpit?

"That's where he hid your input?" I have the urge to check my underarms now. Matthew smiles and shakes his head as if he's reading my mind.

"Better than my groin," he teases.

I have to agree with him there. Matthew approaches me with the other end of the cable, asking permission. I nod and his fingers run gently through my hair until he reaches the spot of the "implant" which would make sense.

When Matthew slides in the plug, it makes me a little queasy; the sensation is just odd. He massages my neck after connecting to me, as if in understanding. We make eye contact then and I let myself soften under the soothing touch. The gray of his eyes is dark with concern.

"Are you ready?" Matthew seems jumpy, like he wants me to change my mind. I can't chicken out of this. More information will help me figure out what to do, who to trust. I can't afford to hide from this. I nod again and the world stops.

Chapter 16

Matthew

The stack of folders mocks me. That Exordium still has paper processes at all, when there were digital options, still makes no sense to me. But there is so much pushback when it comes to changing the littlest of things that I have learned to pick my battles. I've learned a lot about picking my battles lately; a certain smart-mouthed blonde comes to mind.

Every paper I have to read slows me down. I have the ability to understand full databases and spreadsheets in seconds. When it comes to things on paper, I am restricted to what I can read line-by-line. It's frustrating that I can't use that reasoning with anyone else. Only one person now knows the struggle it is for my patience to read physical papers, and she submits every single thing she can in a paper format.

The thought makes me sigh. Charlotte Simpson, the bane of my existence. I feel like I'm cursed. As if I'm in one of the old stories humans tell, fairy tales. The one person who knows what I am, who fascinates me to distraction and makes me feel the oddest sensations, is the person who hates me.

Strong emotions had confused me at first, and sometimes still do. Feeling happy or disappointed is fine but as soon as the outliers hit, everything got fuzzy. What is fury? Is it a burning aggression? A lashing of violence? Why are those also the sensations of lust?

What is the name for the binding sensation in your chest that tightens until you can't breathe, is that pain or love?

I feel like I know what hate is, this urge to bare your teeth and destroy everything in your path. Clark had the ability to bring hate out of me quickly. Is that how Charlotte feels about me?

We haven't spoken in over a week. Somehow, it's possible to work and live in close proximity without contact. I had left it alone because I don't have the first clue about how to diffuse whatever bomb is ticking between the two of us. I am getting worried though. We don't speak, but I watch her.

Humans would probably be disgusted, but I looked up the definition for stalking and I am performing well below that boundary. Whenever I see Charlotte, I watch her. Lately she hasn't been looking right. As if the entire world merely moves around her; like the fire that makes her spit out whatever insults at me has gone out. It had been my intention to ambush her today but when I saw her, she was smiling for the first time in weeks and I had decided to put off our confrontation.

I had more than enough on my plate without prodding Charlotte into a battle of wills. The paperwork stares back at me and despondency closes in on me. It's starting to get dark and it's going to be another long night before creeping back to the apartment building where I can hear Charlotte move from across the hall. The sounds comfort me. I'm sure if she knew I took any comfort in what she did, Charlotte would figure out how to take it away.

Technically, I can't get physically or mentally exhausted but sifting through the mess Clark Simpson made of his company makes me want to burn the whole thing down. The company itself isn't helping matters much. The pushback to going digital is only a small battle to be fought. Anything proposed is sequestered into endless meetings, picked apart until the bright new thing has so many dull holes in it that it becomes similar to something already done. It is all incredibly tedious and boring.

I did not take the CEO position because I wanted it. I ruthlessly plotted to get this position because it is the best way I can help Charlotte. She doesn't want to deal with me in her personal life. But professionally, without my help at Exordium, the board would have found a way to keep her out. Especially the reptile Parsons. I watched him too. Not that Charlotte will ever thank me for interfering in her professional life or any of the other things I've done for her. Clark's will comes to mind.

As I had many times while being locked in that basement, I had gotten bored and had gone on a digital expedition of hacking whatever I could get into. Lawyer offices should have better digital security. I'd almost discarded the find as unimportant until a chill had raced up my spine seeing Charlotte's name next to Parsons's.

Many times, I've asked myself why I care so much about Charlotte Simpson, but definite answers always elude me. I can only define the moment of my obsession. It had been right after one of Clark's many iterations. My creator was analyzing the code as my systems ran. Clark mumbled as he watched the screen, chewing on an end of his glasses.

This had been a common process except for Charlotte coming down the stairs. She had always disregarded the restriction on the basement, asking Clark if he was coming to dinner. I had looked up at her and it was as if something had clicked into place. Like I was really seeing her for the first time. I could remember the details of that moment with crisp clarity.

The artificial lights in the basement bounced off the blonde hair that had been styled in a messy bun on the top of her head, giving her a halo. Her outfit had been simple: a baggy T-shirt with the name of her college on it. The curves of her lower body had been clearly outlined in yoga pants. But her face made something inside me want to lean closer.

I understood that Clark always skimmed over his daughter's face because of her resemblance to his late wife and I could see it in the shape of her brows, the color of her eyes and curve of her mouth. Lush, that would have been how I would have described her mouth. But there was something more to Charlotte than the lines that were similar to Cordelia Simpson. Something about the way she looked at you, as if daring you to do your worst, made her very person a unique thing. I saw Charlotte and something within the core of my being *wanted*.

Sexual urges weren't new to me. Clark had thought it a great laugh to make a machine that could feel desire, could physically act on it. But this wanting was different, something more. Something beautiful and exciting that made the separate parts of my personality coalesce and for the first time, I felt *whole*. A person.

I must have stared at her for longer than I realized because Charlotte dropped her eyes, which was unusual; she always stared at me. This time though her cheeks flushed. A sound came from my side that broke me from my trance.

Clark looked horrified; he gulped and when he spoke his voice had sounded scratchy. "I won't be stopping for dinner tonight, just put my plate in the microwave."

With that, Charlotte ran back up the stairs. Clark's eyebrows went together in concentration as he typed away at his keyboard.

"Can't have that." And with one keystroke, every wonderful thing that had bloomed within the last few moments died. The loss would have felt devastating but the numbness that pervaded helped. Clark nodded in satisfaction and continued working. He had taken away the sensation, but the memory of the moment remained. I could remember feeling real for the first time.

I waited patiently, I didn't have a choice but be patient, until Clark was done for the night. Then I started to plan, looking over my code myself, creating a work-around for Clark's alterations. I didn't know exactly what had happened, but I wouldn't let Clark take it away.

My obsession makes as much sense as anything else in this world. My feelings for Charlotte might seem complicated, but it was simple in the end. Whatever feeling she brought out in me made me feel like a person. Made the world interesting. Made things in my personality merge into an individual thing instead of a Frankenstein project.

I learned everything I could about Charlotte. Even trying to talk to her when she came down into the basement, but something had shifted between her and me. Instead of staring at me she began glaring. When I tried to talk to her, all I got in return were sneers and insults from her lush mouth. I thought I'd done something wrong until I realized the way her father had started to treat her.

Clark started to bring me into the real world. Show me around at Exordium, delighting in being able to show off his creation without anyone realizing what I was. It started whispers that I was his prodigy, that Charlotte would be passed over when the time came. Even though it was blatantly untrue, except for Charlotte being passed over, according to his will.

Clark hadn't been a very effusive father to begin with, but once he started parading me around it got worse. He spent all of his time working on me or on the company. Tweaking the programming that he thought altered me and changing different parts of my design. Multiple times I witnessed Clark ignoring Charlotte's very presence. It wasn't much of a stretch that that was the reason Charlotte began to hate me. Everything had gotten so much worse after Clark's death.

Even though Charlotte hated me, everything I learned about her and saw only made my indescribable feelings for her grow. Her sharp efficiency, creative problem-solving, and the passion she felt for helping others sparked my admiration.

Now I do what I can in a professional sphere while I watch Charlotte become more distant as time goes on. *Tomorrow*, tomorrow I'll try again to untangle the mess between Charlotte and me.

I don't try to explain away being drawn to Charlotte. I can't describe why it feels like a punch to the gut when I see her, why it's better to face her sneering than her absence. It's one of the few things that I feel strongly about. Human psychology supports that having a purpose yields a better life. It's just unfortunate that my chosen purpose hates me.

My cell began to buzz. Surprise makes my brows lift; the caller ID reads Charlotte. I didn't even think she had my number. I pick up and hear breathing and some echoing background noise. A creeping sensation tickles my synapses; I try to ignore it.

"Charlotte? Are you there?" There is a stutter to the breathing that I can now identify as hers. In the pause before she answers I hear the drip of water. Is that a bathtub? Normally the thought of Charlotte bathing would distract me with uncomfortable urges, but this is different.

"Matthew…" Her words slur, and ice suffuses me.

"Just wanted to say goodbye. I love you." Worry and shock are battling inside me as the corners of my vision darken. Panic, that's what this sensation is.

"Charlotte, what are you talking about?" Her breathing still broadcasts clearly, but she doesn't respond. I've grabbed my keys and am rushing, running past the elevator to the staircase. I'd definitely lose phone service in the elevator and the reception on the stairs is spotty but there. It's late enough that there isn't anyone around and I can fly down the stairs as fast as my mechanics allow.

"Where are you? Charlotte? Charlotte?!" The phone cuts off and I swear, wanting to throw it but restrain myself. I head to her apartment, the first place I can think to check. Getting there is a blur; I break down the door without hesitating. I don't know what I had expected to find but it isn't what I see.

Charlotte's apartment is pristine but dark. The lights have all been turned off except one. I barge into the room that has a sliver of light coming from under the door. The bathroom is bright and multiple inputs run through my systems at once.

The bathroom is silent except for the sound of water dripping from the faucet. I see the splash of red on the floor and stop breathing. Glass crunches under my shoes and I cough in relief that it's wine from a broken wine glass. The relief is short lived when I see my Charlotte.

Charlotte floats in the filled tub, wearing some sort of dress, her skin paler than I've ever seen it and her lips tinged blue.

Everything about this moment is suddenly hideous and my chest is being torn apart. A terrible sound breaks the silence, a tortured animal cry that comes from my mouth, my arms go around her and I haul Charlotte out of the tub. The water clings to her in a perverse way, trying to claw her away from me and soaking my suit.

This can't be real. Not Charlotte, not the spitfire who captivates me, who I pledged to support, to help in whatever way she would let me.

I need to save her. It can't be too late to save her, though I can already feel the cold of her fingers and hear no heartbeat.

Something instinctual tells me that it is too late, but I glance on the counter anyway, cataloging and researching the combination of pill bottles on the counter. It only takes a moment for my world to continue to fall apart because she isn't going to be able to come back.

Charlotte is gone. I won't have tomorrow to figure out a way to make her happy. I won't even get any more moments of her scorn. I won't have any more of her. Something breaks inside me; whatever force has been tearing apart my chest has succeeded, and I scatter into pieces. Pain that I've never experienced before burns throughout my person and I cry.

I hold Charlotte's limp body to mine, holding her in a way I had never been able to before, as I sob and rock. This keening tears at me and it's like I'm dying as well. My hand clutches at her wet golden hair as I put my face to hers and pour out this new grief.

A bump under her hair makes everything freeze. The cranial implant behind her ear. Designed and altered by Clark himself. I remember the files Clark had that had taken me some time of looking through to figure out what they were.

I had committed to telling Charlotte about it. I hadn't forgotten; I'm a machine, I don't forget. But higher priorities had kept me from telling Charlotte of her father's violation.

That violation presented an option now. An option that I am positive Charlotte would reject but that I can't help but clinging to. I'll take her hatred. I'll take whatever she throws at me if I can only have one more day. One more chance.

*** *** ***

Charlotte

I'm on my knees gasping when I come back to myself. I look up at Matthew's face and try to parse everything I'd seen, everything I had experienced. Matthew's arms are held out to me, as if he had wanted to catch me when I went down but had stopped at the last moment. My heart is sore from the memory of his feelings.

I stiffen my spine to keep from throwing myself at Matthew. I want to hold Matthew, tell him everything will be all right, to ironically comfort him in his grief of my death. I know more than I did before coming to Matthew. I need to figure out what happens next without letting my emotions get the better of me.

I stand, ignoring Matthew's outstretched hand and he grimaces.

"Thank you for giving me that." My mouth is dry. Matthew nods and takes a few steps away, focusing on some point away from me. He holds himself stiffly, in a controlled manner, like I am.

"I think you know now that I'd do whatever you requested of me." The way Matthew says it almost sounds mechanical but with the echoes of his emotion in my mind, I know he's struggling. I don't want to keep holding him at arm's length, but I'm not ready to give him what he needs from me.

"I still need time," I say, and Matthew clenches his jaw. I see something that looks like pain on his face, but he nods.

"Can I stay here while you go into work?" I ask. Matthew looks confused.

"You're not going to the office?"

"I think that I deserve a sick day, don't you? I also don't want to spend the time going over everything in my apartment. It feels weird to be at the scene of the crime and all that." Matthew's face clears in understanding. "And you also have the best toys."

Matthew's eyebrows wing up and I realize how that sounds. Blushing, I gesture to the piano, making him snort. The humor softens him. It makes me want to reach out, but I hold back.

"Ah, makes sense. Stay here as long as you like then. I'll let you know when I'm on my way back home."

There is a pause before Matthew goes to leave, turning back at the door. "I'll see you tonight?"

I shrug, which is good enough for him and then I'm alone for the second time this morning. I fall onto the piano bench, crumpling now that I don't need to contain myself. I have a day to figure out what to do with what I know, what I am, before having to face Matthew again.

Chapter 17

I almost forgot about my "date".

My day of deliberation is almost over, which is going more like a pity party, when I remember Jim's threat.

The morning had been filled with playing the piano and staring into space. Matthew's plain white walls stare back at me and I imagine what photographic prints I'd hang on them. I had thought that time would bring clarity to my predicament, but everything seems to get muddled the more I consider it.

The only thing I know for sure is that my new life is worth living. I don't want to disable myself for the sake of principle. Matthew walking around is a technological marvel. Me walking around, what it represents for the possibilities for other humans, is dangerous but... I've been given another chance at life and I am going to take it.

I have a blackmail meeting to get ready for.

* * *

Entering the restaurant after last night's encounter is like a practice in repeat masochism: a different night, a different dress, and very different expectations. But the setting is the same, and the man I'm meeting looks the same. Even if it's now evident just how smarmy he is.

Jim gives me a smile when the server directs me to his table. I keep my face neutral as I sit, waving off the menu. I'm not staying long enough to eat.

"You look lovely, as always, Charlotte."

I tilt my head at him but don't answer. We both know I'm not here for a date. Jim looks like he's enjoying drawing this out, so I stay silent. Eventually the man will tell me what he thinks he knows.

"I think you should reconsider being my source for Exordium stories." A sleazy smile.

I give Jim a bored look, but the fear that had been blinding since I'd received his text starts to recede. Had he been arrogant enough to bluff me into thinking he had blackmail material?

"Who knows the information I could dig up, what secrets I'd find, if I looked hard enough."

Ah, he is arrogant enough for the bluff. Jim is here on a fishing expedition. One I'd inadvertently played into.

Stupid.

I had come because there were secrets I didn't want him to know about. My presence from his vague threat means that now he knows those sorts of secrets exist. *So very rash.* I want to kick myself for falling into this trap. If I don't give Jim something, he'll watch Exordium, Matthew and I by extension, until he finds something worth reporting.

Matthew not being human, me not being human, would make a hell of a story.

I need to give him something. Something that will be big enough that he'll leave us alone but not actually cause damage. Can I feed Jim a story without him realizing it? I never thought I was much of an actor, but Matthew had never known that I'd been infatuated with him so maybe I am better at acting than I know.

"I thought you already had your big story." I crease the napkin in front of me. "Matthew wouldn't want me to go on any more of these dates."

I add the second part in a thoughtless way. Jim perks up, a hound scenting the air, or a fish on a hook.

"Do you always do as Matthew tells you?"

I widen my eyes. The motion feels so exaggerated I'm sure Jim can tell it's an act. Jim's smile grows on his face, a Cheshire cat grin.

"I'm sure the public would be very interested in the real relationship between you and Exordium's CEO." Jim's tone sounds salacious. It's a struggle to keep my face from showing my relief. Instead I make the expected plea of someone found out.

"You can't report about that. What would the shareholders think?!"

The shareholders will undoubtedly think that the board manipulated the story around Matthew to keep them calm. Now they will accuse that Matthew is CEO because we are together. It's a small price that I didn't care about paying.

"I can see the headlines now: *Incest! The Truth About the Exordium Siblings.*" Jim makes hand gestures as if the words are in neon lights. I don't have to fake the horrified look on my face. This story is going to be awful.

"If I could get your comment for the story, Ms. Simpson. How long have you been fucking your brother?" Jim sneers out as if to insult me. My brain stumbles, thinking about last night and the blush on my face is real.

"We aren't related. And I can't comment on that." I stand as if I'm too disturbed and flustered by this conversation. The board is going to be furious, but the story could actually be a relief when it's done being awful. I'd love for people to stop referring to Matthew as my brother. I make a half-hearted attempt at a threat.

"If you print that libel, you'll hear from our lawyers!" That's what they say in the movies isn't it? Jim's smile is a nasty thing.

"It is only libel if it isn't true. How careful have you really been, Charlotte?" I give another deer in the headlights look before spinning around and taking my leave. It takes effort not to smile.

Chapter 18

The moment I reach the floor of my apartment, the electric air tingles along my senses. An indication that Matthew's patience has run out. I still have more decisions to make about the technology and how I feel about him. Seeing his memories went a long way in helping me understand him. The unrestrained pain that had cracked through my whole being when he had dragged my body from the bathtub means something.

It means that Matthew cares. Honestly, I think he loves me. I just don't know if he knows it yet. What I'll do with the knowledge is a matter of internal debate. Unfortunately, every time I try to work through it logically, I hit mental roadblocks.

As the air predicted, Matthew waits, like he waited so many nights, at my door. The dark shape of him in the hallway—an omen. I must have missed his text saying he was on his way home. Tonight, he wears a suit, hands shoved into his pockets, staring me down as I approach. Matthew exudes fury. I can taste it on the air, see it in the stiff way he holds himself. His eyes laser down my dress. Ah, that's why he's angry; he thinks I was on a date.

"Matthew, care to take this inside?"

The tightening of his mouth as I unlock my apartment and lead us in causes my blood to hum. His jealousy tastes delicious, partly because of the ridiculousness of it, but also because it's another declaration of how he feels about me. Now that I look for it, signs of his feelings paint everywhere I turn.

Once in the apartment, I throw my purse on the island and remove my heels. "Do you want a drink?" Stalling this conversation is a pleasure. The tightness of Matthew's jaw could break teeth, but he follows me in as if he can't leave more distance between us. Granted, he gives me more space than I thought he would.

"No, I don't want a damn drink. You went out with him again. After everything that happened between us, you went out with that *bottom feeder*."

Rage flows off him in waves. I don't know what wicked thing I did in a past life for his anger to get me off this way, but it does. I turn, leaning back with my elbows against the kitchen island, lower parts of me clenching when I meet his burning eyes.

"I did what I needed to." My lips twitch when I answer him. Oh, he doesn't like that answer. The man looks like he barely restrains himself from baring his teeth. Tough shit, Matthew had his opportunity to manipulate the chess pieces and now it's my turn.

"I'm supposed to just be okay with you going out with another man. Ask how your date went?" Matthew practically spits the words as he closes the distance between us. His snarling builds a hot whimper of need in me and I bite my lip to hold it in. Matthew's gaze immediately goes to my mouth and I know exactly how I want to settle this argument. Being in someone's head gives one lots of insight to the fascinations of that person.

"Maybe you should ask if I got a kiss goodnight," I taunt as I move close enough to feel the heat coming off Matthew's body. He brings his hand to cradle the side of my jaw in a thoughtless gesture, using his thumb to smear my lipstick.

"He better not have." Matthew's voice deepens. I snake my tongue under his thumb while he's distracted and suck it into my mouth. He hisses in what would have sounded like pain if not for the intense look on his face. He growls his next words.

"Don't fucking push me, Charlotte." His whole body winds tighter as I draw harder on his thumb before releasing it to continue its wet path over my lips. The way his breathing stutters tells me if I look down, I'll see his hardness through his suit pants and the thought makes me even wetter.

"I think you've said something about punishing me before, Matthew. Don't tell me that was all talk? How disappointing."

His breathing abruptly goes shallow and my words fall into the space between us, filling it with promises. Matthew stares at my mouth as if I've caused his mind to glitch; the tops of his cheeks flush.

"Charlotte…" After a moment of tension, the hand that had cradled my jaw slides into my hair, giving it a tug that sets my whimper free. Another moment passes, an opportunity Matthew gives me to back out of the gauntlet I've thrown down. When I just wait for him, he pulls my hair downward.

"On your knees." His voice is raspy, stern in its firmness. I'm on fire; I slowly follow the direction of his fist in my hair and lower myself to the kitchen floor. The bite of the hard floor on my knees makes the whole experience sharper. The forbidding look of arousal on Matthew's face has my thighs squeezing together.

"Just what are you willing to do for forgiveness?" The jangle of Matthew unbuckling his belt has me panting, and suddenly his cock is free. Historically, this activity hasn't been my favorite, but like everything else with Matthew, doing this with him is different. The idea of putting my mouth on him excites me and I lean in to give his straining cock a lick but the hand in my hair stops me.

"Uh-uh, no you don't. This is a punishment, not the dessert part of your date. You don't get to savor this at your leisure."

My panties are soaked at the flinty words. I didn't know I'd like this as much as I do. I knew he was hot, made me hot. But I didn't know that he could make me pant in anticipation to experience part of him in this way.

With one hand on his cock and his other in my hair, Matthew places the tip of his arousal on my lips, a bead of precum joining the lipstick smears. Feeling the erotic mess on my mouth makes me desperate to take what he's going to give me.

"I'm guessing you know how obsessed I am with your mouth from the memories I gave you." He taunts us both by sliding his throbbing cock over my lips again. Jesus Christ, I can hear my heartbeat in my ears.

"Since I've known you, this mouth has taunted me. One minute it's sneering or saying snarky words, the next you smile. I used to only care about getting one of those smiles. It's a frustrating endeavor."

Why is he still talking? I part my lips and lick over the head of his cock, causing us both to groan as I taste the saltiness. He tugs my hair, eyes communicating that there will be retribution. I've never been a patient woman.

"Fuck, are you that hungry for me? I've dreamed of this fucking mouth, of fucking this mouth." He pauses, trying to retain control. I run my hands up his thighs, gripping his pants.

"If it gets too much, tap my leg because otherwise, Charlotte, I'm not holding back." The tone of his voice gets to me and I make a small sound. Matthew leaves his cock on my lower lip before giving my jaw a tap.

"Open," he grits out and I eagerly open as Matthew slowly pushes his hips forward, invading the limited space there with his wet cock. The erotic feel of his hot flesh dragging over my lips makes my eyes roll back in my head.

"Now suck." He's practically growling now. I suck him; his cock is much larger than his thumb, but the action is similar, and I can't help my tongue rubbing his shaft. Matthew begins moving his hips, fucking his shaft through my lips. Small motions at first, as if letting me get used to this configuration, before thrusting farther in, causing me to gag a little and the first sensations of panic spark up my spine.

"Shhh… relax your throat; you can take it, Charlotte. You know what to do if you can't. Flatten your tongue, sweetheart."

Refusing to tap out, I follow his instruction. I let myself believe I really am being punished, that I need to please Matthew to gain forgiveness. As I relax, his next thrust goes much deeper and his grunt of approval makes me headily aware of the slick heat between my legs. I'm so turned on, the light gag on the following thrust makes my body tense and I moan.

"Good girl. You like choking on my cock, Charlotte? Because I fucking love how greedy you are for it." I'm so carried away I don't notice my eyes watering until I feel the tears on my cheeks. Matthew keeps his pace measured, as if drawing out my punishment, and wipes away my tears. The tender action releases something in my chest, some last holdout crumbles. His feelings for me go much deeper than I'd let myself believe.

My eyes well with more tears, but I give myself over to the sensations, falling back on the trust I have in him. The surrender seems more than Matthew can handle, his thrusts increase in pace. This is an activity I want to repeat just based on the sounds he is making. His loud breathing punctuated with snarled moans make my hands fist his pants and my whole body tense.

My body thrums, on edge from this, one touch away from being pushed over. But Matthew makes a deeper moan and the end is near for him.

"Oh fuck. Sweetheart, just like that. Now swallow," Matthew releases an extended grunt, holding my hair fast and thrusts his cock deeper, forcing me to swallow the cum filling my throat. Someday, when I'm not aroused out of my mind, I'd ask him technical questions about sexual fluids, but not today. Today I suck him down, reveling in the unintentional sounds coming from him.

Matthew's chest heaves like he's outrun a wild animal. It takes him a minute to remember to loosen the grip on my hair and slide his cock from my mouth. My breaths saw out of me, my body still tense at the precipice of climax. When Matthew goes to tuck himself away, I make a sound that will cause me to feel shame in the morning. Matthew freezes and looks at me.

The air is free of anger but I'm not sure Matthew has finished punishing me. I look up at him. I must look like a mess: knees spread, smeared lipstick, and face flushed. But

his eyes hood in arousal so I must look like a mess in a good
way.

I squirm as Matthew watches me. I don't know what he's
waiting for, then I do. He wants me to beg him. I shouldn't,
I should keep my pride, but an insidious, weak part of me
knows that something as simple as my pride is a small price
to pay for the pleasure he can give me.

"Please—"

Matthew interrupts my plea with a snort.

"You want something from me after what you did?" His
words make my face hot and my chest tight in something
that feels like shame.

"I thought you already punished me. If I were human, my
throat would be sore tomorrow." I pant out the words and
Matthew's face gets a fierce look that only makes me squirm
more. His look turns considering.

"I think you like the rough treatment," he says. I blush.
The rough treatment produces a heady sensation in me. I
don't want to spend hours talking about it, but I'll admit
that part of the reason I push Matthew has to do with how
growly and forceful he gets. Matthew clocks my reaction
and his mouth pulls into a sinful smile.

"Maybe your punishment is leaving you without."

That snaps me out of it. *Asshole.* My hands slide up my
thighs, ready to ease my own ache and show him I don't
need him. I give a frustrated shriek when Matthew picks me
up off the floor and brings us to the couch, sitting with me
on his lap.

"No, you don't. We need to talk, remember?" His voice
sounds teasing.

"I can't talk like this. I can't even think." It comes out in
an unflattering whine, but Matthew looks gratified by my
response.

"I could be convinced to offer you a little relief."

The warmth in his sardonic tone intoxicates me.

"Just so we can get to talking about all those important things that have been tormenting you." Matthew adjusts me to straddling him and moves my hips, grinding on one of his thighs. The rough fabric of his pants is a loud sensation against the wet lace of my panties.

"Your pants will get ruined." I can already tell my panties won't be enough to stop my wetness from making a mess. Matthew's nostrils flare at this statement.

"Fuck the pants."

The need in me, egged on by his response, weakens my control of my motions and I grind against his thigh.

The friction in that first drag is freeing in a way. It doesn't free me from feeling shame at my weakness, rather it frees my desires from where I keep them trapped, exposing them for Matthew. It doesn't matter that I'm unable to stop myself from chasing the feeling because he already knows what I want. Matthew's grip on my hips ratchet up the motions.

"Can't you just fuck me?" I gasp. That would be less shameful than this. Matthew shakes his head slowly, as if drugged.

"Not before we talk. God, you're so wet I can feel it through the pants you're so concerned about."

I don't think about the pants anymore. They are a textured step on my way to absolution.

"That's it, watching you like this is a gift in and of itself," he says. Matthew watches me avidly. His gaze is a physical thing. He watches the dark spot I make on his thigh and the movement of my breasts threatening to pop out of my dress. His gaze spends the most time on my face. My mouth gets the most attention there, my lips feel swollen, tender from abuse.

How long do I move mindlessly on him? It can't take long. My soft parts against his rough. Matthew's analytical gaze forces a fire to burn through me until the pleasure mounts and climbs. All at once my body is seized by a familiar force and I break under a wave of sensations.

My limbs are languid when I return from the mindlessness of oblivion. The first thing that I register is Matthew's face. His expression resembles that of someone seeing the newly completed Sistine Chapel for the first time. Not to compare myself with an artistic masterpiece, but it's hard to remember that I'm not something fantastical when he looks so full of fervor and peace.

We stay there for an immeasurable moment, absorbing each other in this raw moment of time. When the strength comes back to my body, I do what feels like the most natural thing and don't question it. I lean forward and kiss him gently, an odd thing for the two of us, and I rest my head against Matthew's shoulder and cuddle into his space. We hold each other like that until the silence is broken by his ragged sigh.

A wealth of feeling in that single sigh, rich and textured, I let it wash over me instead of deciphering it. I just enjoy the warmth of his body against mine in the rare soft moment.

"I didn't go out with that bottom-feeder because I wanted to." My words come out near a whisper. Matthew makes a rumbly sound.

"How was I supposed to know that? It wouldn't be the first time you've avoided me in a creative way," Matthew says. I sigh, thinking of the terribly immature "pranks" of a past life. As recent as a couple days ago anyway.

"It isn't like that. He made it sound like he knew something. He threatened that I'd be sorry. I was afraid that it was something about you. And well... now me." My voice sounds small and the rigidity of the man under me communicates his unhappiness.

"And you thought that of course you should go and confront him alone." Really unhappy. "You doubted that I could keep us safe."

Matthew's tone doesn't leave room for debate. I poke him, hard. Making my argument anyway. "Our safety isn't just your responsibility. I admit that I didn't approach the problem in a great way; I had a lot on my mind at the time."

"Speaking of..." He starts to draw circles on the flesh of my exposed thigh. The soft touches calm me even with where this conversation is going. Snuggling deeper into his neck, I give a frustrated huff.

"I don't know what to do. I keep running the problems around in my head, but I don't get anywhere with it."

"How about we start with what you know you want to come out of this. We can work backward from that." His plan seems so reasonable.

"I want to be with you –" I start. Matthew's breath of relief cascades through his body. I assume it's because it now goes without saying that I do, in fact, want to stay alive. "I don't know if you feel the same way anymore with the way I've been dragging my feet."

Matthew makes an annoyed sound. "Don't be dense, you've seen inside my head. What about that experience makes you think my desire for you is fleeting?"

"That was before we really got to know each other. You were just watching me. We hardly spoke."

I don't know why I'm fighting him on this. I should just accept that he wants to be with me, but some insecurities won't stay hidden.

"What about our activities tonight, or last night for that matter?" he asks.

"That's sex. Sexual compatibility isn't the only thing required for a relationship."

Matthew mumbles something under his breath that sounds like *fucking stubborn woman*. He jostles me until we're eye to eye, his hands holding my shoulders like he wants to shake me.

"Charlotte Simpson. No one else frustrates me and fascinates me like you do. I'm obsessed past the point of reason, of all logical explanation. Everything stopped mattering to me when you died. When your heart stopped, I might as well have died too for as much as I cared. I recreated your body exactly. You are singular in my universe. Please assume that I'm fully invested in having you be my other half."

I sniff, trying to seem unaffected. "That's a fancy way of saying boyfriend." And incredibly romantic. If I had any walls left to protect myself from Matthew, they would be gone now.

"We can start at boyfriend, if you want. Just know my feelings toward you are not casual." Neither of us have said anything about love. I haven't because my emotions feel scattered every which way. I don't want to rush anything right now. And Matthew… who knows if he recognizes the feeling enough to proclaim it?

The way he felt about me in his memories… from the moment he saw me on those basement steps to when he pulled me out of the tub, he's loved me. It defies all sense, but if he says he feels the same even after we've gotten to know each other, then I need to trust him. It settles my worries and I'm ready to go on to my other topic.

"I want the replacement organ project. I know you don't agree with it," I say. Matthew shakes his head, interrupting me.

"Let's table that issue for now. Don't think about how I feel about the project." That hadn't sounded like a no. Now, on to a topic I don't want to talk about.

"I'm hesitant to bring this technology out. The technology that made me. It feels dangerous. It has the power to change everything. A class war, like you said. People could feasibly live forever. We can live forever! Is that something we should do since we are capable or is that something that shouldn't be done?"

Matthew runs his fingers up the back of my scalp, soothing me, before softly kissing my forehead. The gentle gestures melt the circles of my worries.

"Stop borrowing trouble; you're supposed to be listing the things you know you want to come out of this."

I think about that for a second. "You and my project." They seem like insignificant wants in the face of all the possible outcomes.

"That's it?" Matthew looks surprised.

"There are a lot more things I'm not sure about, than what I am," I say.

"I have some ideas about your project. How do you feel about Exordium as a company?"

I pause, the shifting of my priorities about the company solidifying.

"I don't care about Exordium." I say it almost in wonder, as if I'm released from some sort of compulsion. Matthew nods but I'm still marveling at my change of heart for a company that I had devoted myself to wholeheartedly. "Is that a problem?"

Matthew is the CEO of the company that I no longer had a vested interest in. Matthew answers, "Getting your project approved through Exordium is possible but it will be like paddling in rapids, upstream. The fight will be constant."

"What about the future stuff? The technology? Should we have kids?"

Matthew coughs and raises his eyebrows in surprise. "Maybe we should get a dog first?"

My face heats. I try not to reflect that I just went from accepting Matthew's feelings for me to asking him about kids. I poke him again. "That is not what I meant, and you know it! I'm talking about the ethics of the situation. If we adopted kids would we be ruining their lives? Would we tell them about us? Do we tell anyone? Are we planning to live forever?"

I can't seem to let go of my anxiety.

"I suggest we not worry about everything else and just focus on the items you are sure about," Matthew proposes smoothly.

I shake my head, "So, what? You want to just avoid talking about the future and deal with the now? If we fail to plan –"

"We plan to fail. Yes, I am aware of Clark's favorite, unoriginal, saying. There are so many factors to consider that we have no control over. I'm saying that we should focus solely on the things that we know we want, what we have control over, and leave other decisions until they have to be made."

"How can we make logical decisions if we leave them until the last minute?"

"Life isn't logical." Matthew takes my most utilized tool and discards it. "Life is messy, and some might even say crazy. Trying to make everything logical is futile."

I want to argue but stop. The biggest reason I've fit myself into logic over all else has been to hold on to my own mental health. If I'm not as in danger of spiraling downward, if I have sufficient enough support, do I need to protect my sanity so vigorously with logic?

"Now, my ideas on your project—" Matthew starts in and we stay like that throughout the night. Discussing what options are open to us to make my dream project become a reality. There are upsides for neither of us needing to sleep.

Chapter 19

When the story breaks it's much uglier than I expected. I don't know which paper Jim worked for, it doesn't matter, like dominos one story spurred another and another until even the most respected papers picked it up. The headlines ranged from focusing on that Matthew had been misrepresented by Exordium to appease shareholders to a full incest sex scandal.

So messy. The whole scandal spread through the media streams like a metastasized cancer. I followed the progression for about an hour before forcing myself to put down my tablet. The logical conclusion is that *everyone* knows.

The public backlash is only beginning to be felt. I dispassionately ponder why the idea of incest, where none exists, makes national headlines when *Game of Thrones* had been so popular. But that feels like a topic to be avoided in the upcoming board meeting. The emergency board meeting that had been scheduled for the first thing in the morning.

Luckily, Matthew and I were already in the building. Matthew had set up a meeting for later today, anticipating that the board would need to have their hands held when the story came out. We both had underestimated just how viral the news would go.

A certain associate demanded the meeting to be held earlier so that Matthew and I could be "dealt with". That Parsons had included that in the board-wide email signaled the beginning of a coup. The majority of the board would probably still vote to keep Matthew as the CEO if the subject is raised, but the same majority could vote to remove my seat.

I'm not worried about repercussions. Matthew and I went through all the possibilities when we strategized last night.

"This is outrageous! The two of you couldn't keep it in your pants for the sake of the company?" Parsons looks as if he is half a step away from a heart attack. His bulbous face is deep red, conveying his rage as much as the spittle flying from his mouth.

The members of the board sit around the boardroom table in their scratchy suits and eerily similar features. They look like they are related, with their thin mouths and beady eyes. The expressions on their faces range from disgust to annoyance.

Why was I ever so invested in this company?

I had been so driven to uphold my father's legacy. I would have done near anything that this company had asked of me because it would have been an extension of what Clark Simpson would have wanted.

With the revelation of the depravity with which my father operated his personal business, I'm free. But until I sat before these men, looking down their patronizing noses at me, it hadn't clicked that my ideals and Exordium's ideals will never align.

This isn't my family and I don't owe them anything.

Matthew reaches out and grabs my hand. We had seated ourselves next to each other because there had been no mystery what this meeting was going to be about. Matthew gives my hand a squeeze before smiling a cold, predatory smile at Parsons.

"We're together because it is what makes us happy. You were told the family angle wouldn't work when I became CEO, but insisted on publicizing it," Matthew says. I decide to cut in to avoid the conversation devolving further.

"You don't have to worry about a vote. I'm leaving the company," I say. The faces around the table look relieved at my proclamation. It drives home how unwelcome I am here. Exordium is my father's company in life and throughout death, filled with people who agreed with his ethics and methods. This place isn't my home.

"I'm also leaving," says Matthew. If my statement was supposed to calm the masses, Matthew's statement is the destructive equivalent of dropping a bomb. The change of facial expression around the table to gasping horror is comical and my lips curve. "You get to do with Exordium exactly what you want. We're starting our own company."

Matthew's confidence sings through the room as he announces what we stayed up planning. The silence in the face of this surprise is quickly broken, as expected, by Parsons.

"With what funds?!" Parsons blusters, his white salesman hair waving at his extreme agitation.

"Not that it is any of your business, but we happen to have some investors lined up for it." Matthew's smile never wavers. If anything, I think he's enjoying this more than he should. I know I'm enjoying it, but I deserve to.

I had also been surprised that Matthew had already begun amassing investors in anticipation of my project.

Having the forethought that going through Exordium for it would be a nightmare.

"We will not let you benefit off the back of Exordium! Starting a competing company using connections you got here is unethical! We'll sue you!"

Parsons puffs his chest out at his dramatic declaration. I'm torn between wanting to laugh at his idea of ethics and being concerned that they do have legal ground to stand on. But Matthew just gives Parsons a sly smile.

"I would suggest you look through the paperwork then; trust me, I have." Matthew's voice turns deadly. "Our endeavor and funding are perfectly legal. If you doubt me, take it to your lawyers."

Whispers start to fill the conference room.

With the verbal slaying of Parsons complete, Matthew and I leave the room. Letting the rats behind us begin their scurrying. I think of the way Parsons looked as we stood up; the look of hate clearly broadcast past his usual appealing mask and I have to keep myself from skipping to the elevator.

I pull Matthew into the elevator and hit the floor for his office, allowing the doors to close before pulling him into a kiss that surprises him. I'm wired, heartbeat echoing in my ears. I barely feel the kiss at first until it deepens and Matthew moans into my mouth. When I break off the kiss, my body hums.

"I love you," I say. I start to laugh at the look of absolute shock on Matthew's face. The elevator opens and I dart out toward his office. It doesn't bother me that he doesn't say it back. Our relationship isn't one that would be depicted on rom-coms, but a tangled thing. Weaving in its complexity, beautiful in the simplicity of it. Matthew's feelings for me are no secret, whether he says the words or not.

I still don't expect the crash of Matthew slamming and locking his office door after he follows me in. I don't expect the feral look on his face as he approaches me. I had waved the red flag in front of the bull and ran.

We are back in Matthew's office, an echo of that first day when he asked for my friendship. But this time I run behind the desk, laughing. Teasingly staying out of his reach as he trudges after me.

"People will talk." My smile is too wide for Matthew to think that I really mean that as an argument. Matthew catches me behind the desk and pulls our bodies together before his mouth comes down on mine. I hum and savor him on my lips. He breaks the kiss.

"Everyone is already talking. Maybe we should name our company some reference to incest. We'd already start with so much publicity," he says. I gag and Matthew's chest shakes from his laughter. "No?"

"I hardly think our investors would appreciate that." Not to mention I'd move to a different country to get away from the incest joke if it wasn't a worldwide phenomenon. The best thing to do would be to just work through it. It will get old eventually. I hope.

Matthew sighs. "You're right."

Matthew brings his arms up around me and I narrow my eyes at him for looking so disappointed. His mouth twitches. "This is the last time I'll be in a big boss office like this. I think that calls for a celebration." His mouth is on mine again and I let the kiss move through me as Matthew presses me against the big boss desk.

"A celebration? Do you mean a christening?" I snicker, too lighthearted in happiness to care about being cheesy.

"Ah, but a christening is a ceremony decreeing something ready for use. We're never coming back here so we can't christen this desk." His literal thinking makes me smile. The topic hasn't distracted him to the point of him stopping the press of me against the desk, so I don't take issue with it.

I could say that we are christening the relationship between us. Say something that will make this moment mean something more symbolic than desecrating the desk. But this moment is already more significant in a way I don't want to state with words. Happiness swathes me tight and I'm filled with hope and promise.

This moment starts our new life together. I told him that I love him. Now I want to show him.

I slide to sit on the desk, knocking over something behind me and the plinking sound of scattered pens has me smiling. I spread my legs, a difficult feat with the pencil skirt I wear. The fabric stretches around my outer thighs, cutting. Matthew looks at it with such violence that I intercept his hands on their way to the fabric.

"You will not rip this skirt!" I screech. Matthew chuckles, but I am not walking through the building with a ripped-up skirt. I close my knees and start pulling the skirt up.

Impatient, Matthew begins helping me. I hear some stitches pop at the unforgiving way he yanks the fabric upward but with every inch of sensitive skin exposed, scraped by the wrench of his efforts, I care less and less. With relief the skirt goes to my hips, allowing my legs to fall open and Matthew is there.

The chill of my bare thighs contrasts with the heat of his body pressing into mine. The steel bar in his pants makes my head fall back at contact. The pressure is blissful. Matthew groans as he grinds into the cradle of my thighs.

"Your pants—"

"You and my damn pants," he interrupts me.

"Do you really want to walk out of here with me smeared all over the front of your pants? Don't you think we'll have enough stares already?"

"Let them stare. I want to see you come again just from the feel of me."

I scowl at him. I'll let him boss me around later. There will be many more moments like this going forward. Determined, I grab at his belt, undoing it and pushing his pants out of harm's way before grabbing his fabric-covered erection. Matthew hisses at the contact and pulls my hand away, restraining it as he bites my lip.

"I don't want to go fast this time."

Leave it to Matthew to want slow sex in a daring situation. The door is locked but neither Matthew nor I are technically employed by Exordium anymore. Security could already be on their way up to escort us from the building. But when he gives a slow roll of his hips against my intimate parts my body poses a revolt from saying anything that would make Matthew stop.

"Okay." My exhale is shaky and the look on Matthew's face is devilish. I feel his hand run up my thigh, the calluses of his hand catching on my skin giving me the shivers. The hand moves higher and higher until his thumb presses against my clit, making me gasp. The pressure is a sweet candied thing that makes my mouth water as Matthew's thumb moves in soft circles over my most sensitive area.

The waves of sensation flow over me, making me feel empty. Matthew sucks my bottom lip into his mouth and we're kissing again. Long drugging, wet kisses. We rock, either from my body's eagerness or the movement from the kissing, pressing his thumb harder against me. The sharp sensation has me gasping into his mouth. It hurts but I want more. Matthew is the only one I want hurting me.

Matthew's thumb eases back and I feel the claw of his other fingers as they grab the crotch of my panties; the ripping sound makes me jump. I snap out of the reverie that he has lulled me into.

"Are you fucking kidding me?" The air against wet flesh makes me want to whimper, but the destructive attitude Matthew has toward my property is starting to annoy me.

"You didn't say anything about the underwear. They were in the way."

My lips get nipped again and it's difficult to hold on to my anger in the face of a teasing Matthew.

"What if I made you walk out of here commando? How much would you like that?"

Matthew looks like he's considering it. Maybe he's never been commando before. Who knows the intricacies of male behavior? I don't. I'm also losing my desire to keep on this topic now that my anger has washed away like cheap sidewalk chalk.

I'm spread, wet, and so empty. I don't mind the idea of slow sex but need burns in the back of my throat and everything feels heavy. I pull my hand from Matthew's and use both hands to push his boxers down, releasing his ruddy cock.

Seeing it in the light of day makes me realize I haven't spent much time really looking at it. Face fucking aside, I now run a hand over it. Testing the texture and hardness. It isn't exactly like an organic cock, though I'm no great expert. The artificial skin is softer than expected at parts, but the presence of some ridged underlying veins make my pussy clench.

I massage one of the ridges thoughtfully. "I really like how this part feels inside me."

My conversational taunt doesn't spur Matthew into action. He just tightens his hands on my thighs, waiting out my inspection. He holds himself still until I experimentally give his member a pump. At that, he can't stop his hips from moving in response and a noise comes from the back of his throat. I look up and give him my own devilish grin, enjoying this playful sex edged with intensity.

Matthew's face meets mine and the drugging kisses begin again, but this time I get to control the pace we go. From our mouths tangling in lethargic, sweet kisses to intense devouring kisses all with a slight squeeze and tug of my hand. Matthew growling into my mouth signifies an end to our game.

I move the head of his cock to my opening, rubbing it there to wet it. Matthew breaks the kiss to rest his forehead against mine as he slowly rocks into me. I'm so primed from all our silent promises that the feeling of him entering me has my toes curling and my breath coming in pants.

So wet. So wet that Matthew slides all the way in, first try. His slide is so slow, when he is fully inside me, we both curse and moan. The easy in and out motion is as erotic as me looking down to see the thrust of his cock disappear inside me. A small sound escapes my mouth as I tighten my intimate muscles around him, making the easy, rolling movement of his hips stutter. Matthew puts his mouth next to my ear as I continue to watch where our bodies join.

"You like watching me fuck you? Like seeing how wet you're making my cock?" His words are throaty in my ear.

"Yes." My response is soft and needy. Matthew must like it because the next roll of his hips ends in a punch of force that makes me release a high pitch sound. Our eyes lock together. I pull his face to mine and the kiss I take is a violent thing compared to the earlier sweetness.

With the sting of my teeth, Matthew snaps. His body conquers mine like an act of war, the hard thrusts direct and demanding. The desk starts to rattle with each mighty thrust and it just builds the intensity.

"We need a desk like this at our new company," Matthew snarls tightly.

"More moving, less talking about furniture choices."

Matthew looks me in the eye and slows his pace until the drag of his flesh inside me makes me want to cry.

"Please don't stop!" I'm clawing into his shoulders, ruining his glamorous suit.

Matthew's laugh at that is sharp and short before he resumes fucking me. His next words are a rasp.

"Oh Charlotte, there is no stopping this." His words make me close my eyes in relief. The hard feel of him deep inside me makes me delirious as my pleasure grows.

My body strings tight and my hands start to claw his back. Matthew matches my ferocity as we both climb the frenzy, our bodies come together with a fury. A destructive storm, I break like a crack of lightning, Matthew's groan the thunder. The echoes of our gasping come down like drops of rain.

I rest my forehead against his, holding his body to mine. Thinking words I never thought I would. *I love you.*

After a brief cleanup session, that doesn't do enough to disguise our activities to keep me from blushing under the watchful eye of the security guards, we leave this hollow place and go home. To the home we are going to have together. I'm not concerned with us going too fast. This isn't some random guy I went out on a date with, this is Matthew.

We choose my apartment because it has a bed. As fun as fucking on a desk is, a bed is more comfortable. We repeat the physical affirmation of the love we feel for the rest of the night before dozing in the relaxed way of people who temporarily don't have anywhere else to be. I discover that though we don't need to sleep, it is still a pleasantly relaxing activity. Especially curled up with Matthew.

It's after a long period of "sleep" that Matthew's voice breaks through my fuzzy thoughts. He's running his fingers through my hair, disrupting his position as my big spoon.

"I think I love you," he says under his breath. He thinks I'm still sleeping. *Chicken shit.* I hum and he jumps behind me.

"Maybe drop off the 'I think' part when you say it to me again." I'm enjoying teasing him, but his arms come around me again and he pulls me into a tight embrace.

"I love you, Charlotte Simpson." I smile because everything feels perfect. Neither of us have answers for the long-term, but we're in this together, and we'd figure it out as we go.

Epilogue

The deep sapphire of my evening gown looks amazing against the black of the piano. I let my fingers flow over the keys, the string of music pulling at my heartstrings, like it always does. I wonder if this was how my mother felt during her performances. Wrapped in a fancy gown as she conjured music from her own heartstrings. I bet that even though she was in front of a faceless crowd, she would have felt like she was absolutely alone, her spirit filling the air.

Matthew's hand on my bare back makes me jump and I come back to reality. The music notes fade away, but my heartstrings aren't safe. Matthew smiles down at me.

"I didn't want to interrupt but we have places to be." Matthew in a business suit is a dangerous thing. Matthew in a tuxedo is enough to make me pray for mercy. My mouth goes dry.

"Are you sure we have to go? You're looking very nice."

Matthew's eyes heat at my open perusal but his mouth firms. "I assume you look ravishing; I haven't let myself really look at you because it's our own party and we can't be late."

"It would be so tacky." I wiggled my eyebrows, my tone suggestive. "It's a part of your job to check my dress and tell me how I look."

Matthew looks down, taking in the blue concoction that my stylist said could stop a grown man's heart and I had to be grateful that nothing so trivial could stop my husband's heart from beating. It has been a little over a year since the revelation that my heart beats in the same mechanical way that his does and I have never regretted choosing to continue this life.

"Absolutely beautiful." Matthew's voice is reverent. He sits next to me on the piano bench, kissing my bare shoulder. "Just what a part-owner of Haddell Innovation should wear to celebrate the premarket approval of its first device."

It is a major accomplishment that has taken no small amount of work. The road to develop the Synthetic Respiratory System (SRS) has been bumpy. The challenges of converting a mechanical system into something that could function with a biological system has turned out to be minor compared to the issue of funding.

The majority of funding fluctuated, with stability being elusive until we stopped going to investors looking for a big pay out. Because Exordium had been right, there would be no big pay out for this type of product.

Instead, we started to appeal to the communities in most need of synthetic lungs. Everyone was shocked that crowd funding had worked for a medical device, but it was also a feel-good story. So many people who had originally sat at hospital bedsides feeling helpless in the face of a loved one's struggle were reborn as effective marketing individuals. Utilizing their networks to spread the word and leverage donations. The world is a small place and the vast majority of people know at least one person who could benefit from the technology.

This is a big day for all of those people who have worked so hard. The loved ones of those marketing powerhouses would now be able to get the SRS transplant, extending and increasing quality of life.

Tonight's gala has a two-fold purpose, to celebrate this device's approval and to raise the money required to implement it. It seems counterintuitive to raise money by putting on a costly event but the nonprofit foundation that worked with Haddell Innovation's PR team had already notified us that the donations from the event have raised enough to help all those on the lung transplant list who have chosen the synthetic option.

Some of the event goers are those turned marketing individuals. They will be there to celebrate a hard-won success and were given spots at the gala as a thank you. The rest of the seats have been purchased by those wanting to support the cause in a financial way.

We have our critics. There have been arguments that if the same amount of support is put toward gene editing research that those with genetic issues won't need to get synthetic replacements. But the community sees that solution as one that is far from now and has chosen to endorse the SRS. We wouldn't have been able to make the SRS a reality without that community.

The gala isn't the way I would have chosen to celebrate but it's what our supporters wanted. That, and the added benefit of being able to finance those who needed the SRS, makes getting into a pretty dress worth it. The piano had beckoned me while I had been waiting for Matthew to get off the phone with manufacturing. As always, the music had a way of bringing hidden emotions and thoughts to life.

"Something on your mind?" Matthew looks at me with soft eyes and I blink. I've been staring into space. We have become very good at reading each other. After leaving Exordium we moved in together and Matthew had proposed in short order. I was resistant at first, trying to tell him that everyone would think it was too fast.

"My love for you is not, has never been, a temporary thing. This is the one area where I don't give a shit about what people think." His words had made me nod because he was right. Our relationship will never be like other people's.

I hadn't held out for long and we had a small private ceremony the following week. Neither of us had cared about a fancy wedding and the press would have turned it into a circus. Now, after a year of trials and tribulations, the press rarely brought up the incest thing. The dealings at Haddell have been much more interesting, thank goodness.

I don't know how to repay Matthew's indulgence in allowing me to name our company for Sean. It's fitting since Sean's family helped with funding and his sisters make a badass PR team. So many things have come together to make this project a reality and now it is done. There will still be things to refine about it, but the product is developed. This milestone is huge.

My thoughts lead me back to the present moment.

"Is this the time you want to readdress the hard questions? My feelings have not changed about the technology that preserved your life as I'm sure you would agree. After this whole process with the SRS project I'm okay with innovation done responsibly. It's hard enough to get people to accept a synthetic option when their life is on the line so I'm not concerned that humans will flock to immortality." Matthew is right. There is a percentage of patients who refused the SRS option even though it